SOME...
DEATH FOR T...

A lot of people loved Roger Parnell. His sensational good looks, easy charm, and overflowing wallet worked wonders, especially with women.

A lot of people hated Roger Parnell. A jealous husband . . . a spurned lover . . . an indignant parent . . . an outraged teacher . . . a swindled client . . . a nervous business partner. . . . There were at least a dozen people who wanted him dead. Which of the sensible citizens behind the well-trimmed hedges of exclusive Petal Park was a dangerous killer?

SPENCE HAD TO WRAP
UP THE CASE BEFORE CHRISTMAS

MURDER INK.® MYSTERIES

1. DEATH IN THE MORNING, *Sheila Radley*
3. THE BRANDENBURG HOTEL, *Pauline Glen Winslow*
5. MCGARR AND THE SIENESE CONSPIRACY, *Bartholomew Gill*
7. THE RED HOUSE MYSTERY, *A. A. Milne*
9. THE MINUTEMAN MURDER, *Jane Langton*
11. MY FOE OUTSTRETCH'D BENEATH THE TREE, *V. C. Clinton-Baddeley*
13. GUILT EDGED, *W. J. Burley*

SCENE OF THE CRIME™ MYSTERIES

2. A MEDIUM FOR MURDER, *Mignon Warner*
4. DEATH OF A MYSTERY WRITER, *Robert Barnard*
6. DEATH AFTER BREAKFAST, *Hugh Pentecost*
8. THE POISONED CHOCOLATES CASE, *Anthony Berkeley*
10. A SPRIG OF SEA LAVENDER, *J.R.L. Anderson*
12. WATSON'S CHOICE, *Gladys Mitchell*
14. SPENCE AND THE HOLIDAY MURDERS, *Michael Allen*

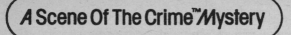

A Scene Of The Crime™ Mystery

SPENCE
and the
HOLIDAY
MURDERS

Michael Allen

A DELL BOOK

Published by
Dell Publishing Co., Inc.
1 Dag Hammarskjold Plaza
New York, New York 10017

Dell ® TM 681510, Dell Publishing Co., Inc.

ISBN: 0-440-18364-2

Reprinted by arrangement with Walker and Company
Printed in the United States of America
First printing—February 1981

SPENCE
and the
HOLIDAY
MURDERS

1

If Roger Parnell had known that he was going to be murdered in two and a half hours time he would undoubtedly have paid more attention to the stripper who was featured in the ten o'clock cabaret at Big Fat Nelly's nightclub.

Parnell was a young man with an experienced eye for strippers, but at that particular moment he was thinking of another girl altogether, a girl whom he had known four years earlier and who was now dead. For a while that evening he had managed to forget her, but when the compère had announced the stripper's name as Jane the memories had begun their instant replay once again—memories which were painful in their implications. He hadn't loved her, that earlier Jane, but she had loved him, and she had come to no good because of it. Roger dragged his wandering attention back to the gyrating hips of the real live girl in front of him and tried to show some appreciation.

For her part the stripper paid a lot of attention to Roger Parnell: he was the best-looking young man in the room, and at first she worked entirely to him; she even blew him a kiss at one point but there was no response. After that she concentrated instead on the only other unaccompanied male in the thin Tuesday night audience, a middle-aged man with glasses, tucked away at one side. But he was a shrinking violet too and gave her no encouragement whatever; she cut her losses, took everything off fast and called it a day. Just not her night, that was all; the one o'clock show might be better.

After the cabaret was over Roger went into the nightclub's restaurant and ordered a steak. He felt better with that inside him and got into conversation with a young couple at a table nearby. The girl said that the stripper's boobs had been pumped up with paraffin; her boy friend thought they were natural; what did Roger think? Silicone, said Roger, and they passed a few idle moments talking about the respective merits of the two materials, and Las Vegas showgirls with fifty-four-inch busts. After that the young couple went off home, to continue the discussion in private, Roger suspected; he himself went into the bar.

He looked around for a familiar face, but slightly to his surprise recognized no one. A middle-aged man with a small moustache and national health service glasses rang a slight bell, but Roger couldn't quite place him and the man was deeply engrossed in an evening paper; he obviously didn't want to talk to anyone.

After a while Big Fat Nelly herself came down the bar for a chat. She was a huge, dangerous-looking woman in a long black evening dress, heavily made up; the upper half of her body was forever wreathed in clouds of cigarette smoke.

'How was the steak?' asked Nelly.

'Fine,' said Roger, without real enthusiasm.

'I only asked,' growled Nelly, 'because you look as though it gave you indigestion.'

Roger grinned; he couldn't stay gloomy for long. 'No, it's not that,' he said. 'It's just that I had a bit of bad news earlier on tonight.'

'Oh. Business?'

'No, no. . . . It's an old girl friend of mine actually. You may know her—a girl called Jane, Jane Trent.'

Nellie thought for a moment, then shook her head. 'No, I can't say I do. What about her?'

'Well, she's just died, that's all. Her best friend came round to tell me just before I came out—apparently Jane wanted me to be the first to know.'

'Charming,' said Nelly. She inhaled deeply, her dark eyes scanning the room. 'What she die of?'

Roger grunted. 'Huh—you name it, she was on it. Speed, coke, morphine, heroin, the lot. Amazing she lasted as long as she did really.'

'Well,' said Nelly, 'if she was that sort I wouldn't know her. She won't have been in here—you know my rules.'

'True,' said Roger. 'True. . . .' He began to feel depressed again. 'Give me another drink, will you?' he said.

Things improved later on. A few acquaintances came in after the pubs shut and Roger chatted away the last hour of his life in congenial company. It was twelve-fifteen when he finally left the club and hurried through the cold December night to his car, a Ford Escort GT. He noticed as he climbed into the driving seat that the middle-aged man in glasses had followed him out of the nightclub and was hurriedly unlocking the door of his own car across the road: it was an anonymous-looking Austin 1100. Once again Roger tried to remember where he had seen the man before, and failed.

It was a ten-minute drive home and Roger noticed that the Austin 1100 stayed behind him nearly all the way. But then when Roger turned right off the London Road into Petal Park Road the 1100 went straight on and Roger relaxed. For a few minutes he had begun to have paranoid ideas about being followed. But nobody would want to have him followed. . . . Would they?

Roger put his car in its garage, closed the doors and walked carefully across the drive towards his front door—carefully because it was very dark, the street lights hidden by a thick hedge bordering the road.

He paused a few feet away from the door to select the right key; it was a process which required some concentration because he had drunk much more than usual. As he stood there he heard a slight sound behind him. He just had time to think that when he had sorted out the damn keys he would turn round and see what it was. But he never had a chance to move: a split second after he thought about investigating the source of that sound, the world exploded into a thousand flaring fragments and an appalling spasm of pain. The keys jerked out of his fingers and clinked against some empty milk bottles. For all practical purposes Roger Parnell was dead before his body slumped on to the asphalt drive.

He was twenty-six years old.

2

Murder inquiries begin at all times of the day and night; for Detective Superintendent Ben Spence this one began at eight-forty a.m. on Wednesday 22 December.

It was eight-thirty precisely when Spence entered the Southshire Police Headquarters in Wellbridge, the county town. He was a tall man with wide shoulders and he was wearing a heavy double-breasted overcoat which made his frame even more impressive than usual. Underneath the overcoat Spence wore a plain grey flannel suit. His father had never worn the same suit two days running, on the grounds that they lasted twice as long that way. Spence had followed his father's example, but he preferred not to let the habit be obvious. He owned three grey suits, all cut from the same cloth, and three blue ones to ring the changes; they all had double-breasted jackets with long vents at each side and deep, reinforced pockets to hold all the debris that Spence seemed to accumulate during the working day. His shoes were black, and specially made in London; Spence had learned on the beat, the hard way, to take care of his feet, and bespoke shoes were his chief extravagance.

Spence was a week past his thirty-eighth birthday,

but still fit enough to take the stairs to his first-floor office two at a time. His dark brown hair, parted neatly on the left, was cut short on the top and left full at the sides and back; his wife made an appointment for him at her hairdresser's every four weeks and instructed the girl how to cut it.

The face was clean-shaven and still carried a light tan, evidence of spare time spent in the open air rather than of holidays taken abroad. His expression was almost invariably cheerful: disgustingly cheerful, some colleagues had been known to call it.

The eyes were brown, and surrounded by clear white; they were friendly enough in most people's estimation, but professional law-breakers had been known to find them unsettling. In his first year as a detective Spence had been taught by an old hand to stare hard at a suspect straight between the eyes; he had thought it a corny dodge at the time but still tried it occasionally when he could think of nothing better; it upset some people no end.

It was eight thirty-five when Spence sat down at his desk. The head of the Southshire CID, Detective Chief Superintendent Booth, had been on sick leave for the past three weeks following a coronary. Consequently the pile of paperwork on the desk was even bigger than usual, and Spence had barely begun to sort through it when the phone rang. He answered it with his name.

'Good morning sir,' said a voice at the other end. 'Laurel here.'

'Oh, and good morning to you,' said Spence. Detective Inspector Laurel was in charge of the London Road sub-division in Downsea, some fifteen miles to the south, on the coast. 'What can I do for you, Mr. Laurel?'

'We've found the body of a young man, sir. I thought you ought to know.'

'I see. Where is it?'

'Outside a house in Petal Park Avenue. That's off the London Road.'

'Hmm. . . . Are you certain he's dead?'

'Yes sir, quite certain. A doctor lives next door and he's confirmed it. He's also identified the victim as the owner of the house, a chap called Roger Parnell.'

'Do you know him?'

'No, sir.'

'Is he married?'

'No, single. No immediate family either, I understand.'

'OK,' said Spence. 'Well, just follow standing orders, put the usual drill into operation and I'll be with you as soon as I can.'

Spence put down the phone, picked up his overcoat and headed down the corridor. 'Wilberforce!' he bawled.

'Yes, sir?' Detective Sergeant Percy Wilberforce appeared at the door of his office almost before the echo of his name had died. Wilberforce had been twenty-two years on the strength and was a man of immaculate appearance and military bearing; he stood with a spine like a plumb-line, a habit which he had developed many years earlier in order to satisfy the height requirement for the force. He wore a brown sports jacket, green trousers with cuffs, and fiercely polished brown shoes. No fancy piece in a mini-skirt ever cut *his* hair: it was short back and sides, Brylcreem and no nonsense; in some lights it looked as though someone had painted his skull with black lacquer.

Unlike most policemen, Wilberforce was never happier than when faced by a mountain of bumph. It was said his wife was a shrew and that he welcomed any excuse for staying late at work; whatever the truth of it, the CID found his capacity for hard work and his talent for mastering a flood of paper extremely useful on murder cases.

'We've got a dead one,' Spence told him. 'Petal Park Avenue in Downsea.' Wilberforce's moustache almost visibly bristled at the news. 'Detective Inspector Laurel is in charge down there, but you'd better get the show on the road from this end.'

'Yes, sir.'

Spence began to pull on his overcoat. 'Put the mobile office round the back of the London Road police station for the moment. And book me into a hotel for the next few nights, it'll save an hour a day. The George will do.'

'Yes, sir.'

'And phone my wife and explain,' said Spence as he headed for the stairs.

'Yes, sir. Certainly, sir. Leave it to me, sir,' said Wilberforce. He meant it, too.

Spence disappeared and Wilberforce went back into his office. He rubbed his hands and danced a little jig. It wasn't that he was a callous man, but there was no doubt about it, a murder case was a bit more interesting than the usual run of events.

3

Spence climbed into his car, a dark-blue Ford Cortina 2000 GT, and began to plough his way through the morning traffic. A lot of people had obviously had the bright idea of coming into town early to get on with their Christmas shopping; what with them and the usual morning commuters the streets were jammed. Spence's car was not overtly identified as a police vehicle but it had a siren fitted, and under the dash-board was a flashing blue light which he could clamp on to the roof in emergencies. But in this density of traffic nothing was going to make much difference, and he decided to be patient. Roger Parnell was already dead, after all.

While Spence was on the road Detective Inspector Laurel was following standing orders to the letter. Until Spence arrived he was in sole charge, and he was anxious not to make any mistakes. There was a whole list of people to be informed: the Chief Constable, the Assistant Chief Constable (Crime), the pathologist appointed by the Home Office, the director of the regional forensic science laboratory, and the County Coroner, for a start. Then there were the lesser lights such as the chief photographer, the chief fingerprint man, and even the civilian who drew plans the way Spence liked them.

On top of all that Laurel had to remember to detain the person who found the body (a milkman), make sure that nobody approached the scene of the crime (not very difficult in this case), and generally try to look efficient. At the last moment he realized that he had forgotten to get a police car positioned on the outskirts of Downsea to guide Spence in, and he spent a few agonized moments making arrangements over the radio. After that he was able to relax a little.

While Detective Inspector Laurel was sweating nervously at the scene of the murder, Percy Wilberforce was arranging for Spence's mobile office unit, all twenty-seven feet of it, to be transported from County Police Headquarters in Wellbridge to the parking lot behind the London Road police station in Downsea. Then there were files, statement forms, envelopes, a blackboard, job cards, carbon papers, pens, pencils, and a thousand and one other things to be put into the right place at the right time.

Wilberforce didn't sweat, though: he had done it all five times before, and after the third time he had got it completely taped. He simply barked his orders into the telephone and men went to work—and if they didn't he would want to know the reason why. In triplicate.

By nine-ten a.m. Spence was on the outskirts of Downsea. He passed the small flour mill which had once been owned by the Spence family and was now owned by a huge combine. After two sets of death duties and division between two branches of the family, not much was left of the proceeds of that sale, but

Spence never thought twice about it one way or the other. He was quite sure that he was happier being a policeman than a miller.

Ahead of him a Panda car moved out of a layby to lead him to the scene of the crime and Spence flashed his headlights in acknowledgement.

Downsea was a posh little town, no question about it, Spence reminded himself. He glanced at the exclusive golf club on the left, and then back at the sea looking green in the distance ahead of him. Nearly all the property in Downsea was expensive and looked it; much of it was owned by retired people. The town formed a wealthy annexe to Shireport, a healthily vulgar seaside resort about two miles down the coast; Shireport was where many of the Downsea residents had made their money. There was a certain amount of light industry in Downsea, glove-making and boat-building for instance, and there were some fine hotels for the top end of the holiday trade. But mostly the people who lived there were the kind who read the *Financial Times* every day, and worried about what it said.

The patrol car ahead of Spence turned left into what he noted was called Petal Park Road; it then turned left again into Petal Park Avenue. The Panda car stopped about two hundred yards up the avenue, just before the road curved to the right; Spence parked behind it and then got out and looked around him.

Besides his own car and the Panda car which had guided him in there were four other vehicles parked in the road, one of them a milk float. No press or television crews could be seen as yet. Spence noticed Detective Inspector Laurel approaching him, but he stayed where he was, by his car, and continued to look around.

The avenue was a broad road, lined with trees, and thick hedges and high fences hid most of the houses from sight. Such houses as Spence could see were detached, probably built at the turn of the century, and doubtless offering at least five or six bedrooms. It was a quiet area, almost oppressively so; only a chattering group of teenage schoolboys on their bicycles gave any indication that the calm had been shattered by a murder.

Funny about those lads, thought Spence. You could tell at a glance that they were public-school boys, home for the Christmas holidays, rather than products of the local comprehensive.

Despite his best intentions Detective Inspector Laurel was feeling distinctly harassed, and it showed; he approached at almost a trot. 'Good morning, sir,' he began. 'If you'd like to come with me I'll show you the body.' He turned and began to pace rapidly away.

'Just hold on a minute,' said Spence firmly, and rather reluctantly Laurel returned.

'Before we go rushing off let's get a few things established,' Spence went on. 'Any specialists here yet?'

'No, sir.'

'But all sent for, I assume?'

'Yes, sir.'

'Good. And you've notified the Chief Constable and all the rest of them?'

'I've left appropriate messages, yes, sir.'

Spence nodded and took a careful look at Laurel while appearing to take in the avenue and the local scenery. Laurel was thirty-five, a widower with two teenage children; he was acknowledged to be an efficient and hard-working officer. Physically the most noticeable feature about him was his gingery hair, which was long enough at the front to flop down over his eyebrows. After that people noticed his nose, which still carried a kink in it from a rugby game some ten years earlier.

Laurel's dark-grey overcoat was neat enough and the black shoes had been polished. But his red tie had been knotted more often than was good for it and the trousers of his suit needed pressing; the left cuff on his shirt was also sadly frayed. All in all, Laurel had the look of a man who badly needed a woman to look after him.

'Right then, Mr Laurel,' said Spence, 'What about manpower?'

'I've arranged for twenty men to be free by twelve o'clock for a briefing—all the detectives I can lay my hands on plus some men from the Regional Crime Squad. They're all expecting to spend the rest of the day on door-to-door inquiries.'

'All right, that'll do for a start. And now you can show me the body.'

They set off towards the gate of a house on the left-hand side of the avenue, the last house before the road made a ninety-degree turn to the right. Just as they were about to enter the drive, however, an ancient grey minivan came roaring up the avenue in third gear. Both men turned to look at it. The van squealed to a halt beside them, and in fact it would clearly have driven right up the drive to the house itself if Spence and Laurel had not been in the way.

The driver, a young woman in her early twenties, leapt out of the van and was about to run past them when Spence grabbed her by the arm and pulled her without ceremony to one side. He turned her round so that her back was to the group of men standing quietly round the still form near the front door.

'Just a minute, young lady,' he said. 'You can't go up there, either with your van or without it.'

The young lady in question opened her mouth and seemed about to argue. But then she looked into Spence's eyes and changed her mind. She took several deep breaths and visibly regained control of herself.

'Oh,' she said flatly. 'So it's true then, is it? Roger really has been murdered.'

Spence was reluctant to answer this question until he was certain that no one had made a silly mistake. But the girl didn't seem to need an answer.

'I'm sorry,' she said, still gasping for breath. 'That was a bit stupid.' She took off her glasses and wiped her eyes. 'I'm afraid I got a bit carried away, charging round here as soon as I heard. . . . But it was a shock, you know. A terrible shock.'

She put her glasses back on and Spence took a mental inventory of her clothes and appearance. She was of average height, and her figure, what he could see of it under an Aran coat, seemed trim enough. The glasses had been carefully chosen for colour and shape, and despite the old saying, they would have done nothing to discourage men from making passes. Her tear-stained face, however, would not have given the girl much pleasure if she had glanced in a mirror at that moment.

'Perhaps you'd better tell me your name,' said Spence.

'Dawn. Dawn Stenning.'

'And you're married,' said Spence, who had seen her hands.

'Yes.'

'Address?'

'The Lodge, Petal Park.' She sniffed and groped for a handkerchief in her coat pocket. 'It's over there, at the entrance to the school.' She nodded in the vague direction of Roger Parnell's house.

'I see. And you knew Mr Parnell?'

'Oh yes.' She blew her nose. 'Yes, I knew him all right. I was quite fond of him.'

Spence wondered briefly whether to get her to enlarge on this last remark but decided that this was not the time or place.

'You were a friend of his, then,' he said.

'Oh yes. Yes, that's right. Just a friend.'

'I see,' said Spence kindly. 'Well, Mrs Stenning, I think the best thing you can do at the moment is go home. It sounds to me as if you might well be able to help us, but not here and now. I'll see that someone comes round to see you later on today and you can tell us all you know. We'll be glad to have your help. How does that sound?'

'All right. . . .' said the girl hesitantly. 'All right, I suppose. I'd—er—I'd better go, I suppose, before I make a complete spectacle of myself.' She smiled ruefully, walked rather unsteadily back to her minivan and climbed in. Spence and Laurel watched as she reversed awkwardly out of the entrance to the drive, and went back the way she had come.

'Hmm,' said Spence. 'I see you're a merciful man too, Mr Laurel.'

'How do you mean?' said Laurel.

'The road fund licence on her minivan,' said Spence. 'It's nearly two months out of date, but I hadn't the heart to do her for it.'

4

Spence sent a uniformed constable to take the names and addresses of the boys who were loitering in the avenue; nothing cleared a crowd quicker than a policeman with a notebook, and sometimes the names were those of useful witnesses. Then he and Laurel went up the drive of the house to look at the body.

As they walked the twenty yards to the front door Spence noted that the one-car garage was to the left of the house and detached from the house itself, with its door closed; between the house and the garage was a passageway leading presumably to the back garden. At the front of the house the boundaries of the garden were marked by thick hedges on all three sides.

'Is there a car in the garage?' asked Spence.

'Yes, sir, you can see it through the window on the far side.'

'What kind is it?'

'A Ford Escort GT.'

'And does it belong to Parnell?'

'Yes, I got the doctor next door to have a look at it.'

'Good.'

The body of Roger Parnell lay quite close to the front door, face upwards, the head not quite touching the doorstep. A pool of blood had followed the contours of the asphalt drive and spread out to the right.

Carefully Spence knelt down on the left of the corpse and began to examine it. To anyone who had been fond of Roger Parnell in his lifetime such proximity would have been intolerable, but already Spence's mind had closed itself off from the emotional implications of death and had begun to work on the problem of who had killed this man, and why.

'Now then,' said Spence, 'one of the first things to learn about working on a murder case with me is that I talk to myself. I think aloud, and I advise you to do the same. That way we shall give each other ideas. Now, let's see what we have here. . . . First the physical appearance. Age, probably middle twenties. Average height and build. Black curly hair, quite long by the standards of my youth. Bright blue eyes, rather fish-like at present. . . . Now the clothes. Short black leather overcoat with belt, unbuttoned. No gloves. Underneath, a dark-grey suit with a pin-stripe, rather modern in style with bell bottoms on the trousers. White shirt with a dark-blue tie. Black Chelsea boots. . . . Overall impression: smart, well dressed, fairly expensively dressed. They look like gold cuff-links. . . . Anything to add?'

'Looks as if he's been in a fight,' said Laurel. 'Someone's given him a couple of black eyes, wouldn't you say so?'

'No,' said Spence, 'I wouldn't. Not in the way you mean, anyway. What's happened here is that someone has bashed him on the back of the skull, as we shall see when we turn him over. What happens when you do that, in some cases at any rate, is that the eyeballs slam forward in their sockets and produce the sort of bruising you can see here. . . . What else do you notice from the way the blood has run down his face?'

Laurel guessed. 'He's been dead some time?'

'Yes, but more important, someone turned him over,' said Spence. 'Shortly after death, I would say. The pathologist will tell us for sure, but that's my reading anyway.' He stood up. 'Well, my first impressions are that he came home and put his car away. He was approaching the front door when somebody came up from behind and slugged him. Whoever did it was probably waiting in the passage between the house and the garage. . . . What sort of light is there here at night?'

'Precious little,' said Laurel. 'The street lights are too far away to be much good and there's no porch light.'

'And there couldn't have been much moon last night,' said Spence. 'Too cloudy, where I was at any rate.'

'There's a bunch of keys over here,' said Laurel.

'Where?'

'Behind these milk bottles.' He pointed.

'Oh yes. . . . They look like car ignition and door keys, a key to the house, and a couple of others. Interesting, that. Perhaps he paused just before the step to select the right key for the front door. And while he was standing there, sorting them out, somebody hit him. Don't forget to get those keys fingerprinted. They probably flew out of his hand when he was hit, but you never know, the murderer may have touched them. . . . Right, well, let's have a walk round the house before the specialists get here.'

Together Spence and Laurel went round to the back

of the house. The asphalt in the drive had been continued through the passageway to the right of the garage, and at the back there was a patio of pavingstones which had clearly been there as long as the house. Neither surface offered the slightest hint of a footprint.

They paused and looked down the back garden. The hedges which guarded the front and sides of the house were continued as far as the end of the garden; but on the fourth side there was a low wooden fence instead of a hedge, just a row of vertical posts with two rails running from side to side. Beyond the fence was a sports field laid out as a hockey pitch, and beyond that a house of considerable size with numerous wings and outbuildings branching from it.

'What's that place?' said Spence.

'Petal Park Girls' School.'

Spence grunted. 'Oh yes. I've heard of it.'

'It's a private school,' said Laurel. 'The Chief Constable sent his daughter there a few years ago and all the local nobs use it. Fees are something astronomical, I believe.'

'So I've heard,' said Spence. 'Let's wander down the garden, see if there's anything unusual. We'll have to get the place searched properly later on but I like to see for myself.'

The two men walked slowly down the path towards the end of the garden, keeping their eyes on the ground for the most part. As they neared the fence which marked the rear boundary of the garden a woman came into view in the playing field beyond. She was about thirty-five, wrapped in a thick winter coat, with an elderly golden labrador at her heels. The woman was looking keenly towards Roger Parnell's house when they first saw her, but when she noticed them she turned her head sharply away and changed direction slightly; instead of walking parallel with the fence she was now walking away from it.

'Just a minute,' called Spence, and the woman stopped. It was clear from her expression that she didn't like being addressed so abruptly but she obeyed none the less. 'I'd like a word,' said Spence. 'I think you might be able to help us.'

The woman joined him at the fence but was careful to stand out of reach. 'Yes?' she said. She tossed the light brown hair out of her eyes as if she were constantly being accosted by strange men and wasn't bothered by it at all.

'We're police officers,' said Spence. He took out his warrant card and offered it, but the woman didn't bother to examine it closely.

'Oh yes,' she said. 'Has there been a break-in?'

'We're making some inquiries here,' said Spence noncommittally. 'Perhaps you can help. Do you often walk your dog around here?'

'Quite often.' The woman looked cold, despite the camel-coloured coat. 'Once a day at least. I live in the school over there.' She pointed.

'Have you seen anything unusual recently?' asked Spence. 'Anyone suspicious hanging about?'

The woman thought. 'No,' she said slowly. 'No, I can't say I have.'

She was single, Spence decided, and educated too. A schoolmarm for sure, rather posh and very tense, but there was nothing in that; men would always disturb her.

'What sort of unusual things do you mean?' she went on.

'Oh, strangers about. Things not where they usually are. Odd noises. Anything at all.'

The woman shook her head, more relaxed now. She tried a helpful smile. 'No, sorry. I can't say I have. But there've been quite a lot of burglaries in the houses round here and I never noticed anything strange all the other times either.'

Spence smiled back at her. 'Not to worry,' he said reassuringly. 'It was worth asking.' He turned to go but then added almost as an afterthought: 'Oh—you're from the school, you say?'

'Yes, that's right.'

'And your name?'

'Leigh—Miss Leigh.'

'Oh, well, thank you, Miss Leigh. What's the dog's name?'

'Him? He's called Goldie.'

'Nice dog,' said Spence. 'You'd better go, he's restless.'

'Come on, Goldie,' said Miss Leigh, and moved off in the direction of the school.

Spence and Laurel came back up the garden path. 'Hello,' said Spence as they neared the house. 'Take a look at this.' He approached a french window which opened into what was obviously the living-room; the panes of glass in it were about twelve inches by nine, and one of them had been broken. It wasn't easy to see from most angles because every scrap of glass had been knocked out of it, mostly on to the living-room carpet. Spence didn't ask if Laurel had noticed it before and Laurel was too busy cursing himself for not having noticed it to comment.

'Looks as if someone broke in,' said Spence. He peered through the window. 'They could have put their hand through the hole here and unlocked the door easily enough—they could reach the key downwards and the bolt upwards. I won't try the handle till the fingerprint boys have been.'

'I can't see any great signs of the place being ransacked,' said Laurel. 'Just a few newspapers lying around. I wonder what they were after?'

'Too early to guess,' said Spence. 'Anyway let's go back. We'll search the house later on.'

At the front of the house the specialist investigators were beginning to arrive. The usual practice in a Southshire murder case was for Detective Chief Superintendent Booth to be in overall charge and for Spence to do the organising and most of the donkey work. Now, with Booth in hospital, Spence was on his own for the first time, but the routine was already well esablished. As far as possible, allowing for sickness and leave, Spence used the same experts on every murder case so that they got to know his requirements. The photographer, for instance, had not only brought along his camera but also hand-held television equipment. He pulled a pair of steps out of his van and began making a videotape of the whole scene, including shots looking down on the body from the top of the steps; he knew that Spence particularly liked a bird's eye view. The fingerprint man started work on the garage and the car, and the man who drew sketches scribbled busily. And whatever they were doing, everybody made room for the pathologist appointed to the force by the Home Office, Dr Dunbar.

Dunbar was in his middle forties; he was wearing a fawn trench coat over a brown sports jacket, cavalry twill trousers and brown suede shoes; a Russian-style fur hat completed his outfit. In Spence's eyes Dunbar always looked like an army officer in civvies; it was something about the way he carried himself, his air of brisk efficiency. And there was certainly no doubt that Dunbar regarded himself as an officer. In fact, in the nicest possible way, he regarded himself as a general; once he arrived on the scene he expected everyone to stand to attention. It was a form of conceit which Spence pandered to only in the interests of securing maximum cooperation. Dunbar had more letters after his name than anyone else at the scene of the crime, and the letters gave a fair indication of the extent and depth of his knowledge; Spence found him a valuable colleague.

Together Spence and Dunbar knelt down beside the body for a conference. It was obvious that Dunbar had done this sort of thing before because he had brought a cushion for his knees.

'Well,' said Dunbar, 'for a start it doesn't look like suicide.' He proceeded to roll back the sleeves of his various garments so that he could poke and prod without soiling them. 'Know who he is yet?' he asked.

'Roger Parnell,' said Spence. 'Lives here, or did. What did he do for a living, Mr Laurel?'

'Director of a firm of insurance brokers,' said Laurel. 'He was a single man, lived alone. . . . The mikman found him about ten past eight. He knew there was a doctor living next door so he went round and fetched him. The doctor decided Parnell was dead, telephoned us and identified him. Then he got on with his surgery.'

'Where's the milkman now?' asked Spence.

'Over at the doctor's—the doc's wife is giving him a cup of tea. I've got a man taking a statement from him, and there's also a cleaning woman over there. She arrived about nine o'clock and I asked her to stay because I thought you'd want to speak to her.'

'I do indeed,' said Spence. 'Have we informed the Coroner?'

'Yes.'

'And what about Parnell's firm?'

'I rang them and spoke to the manager's secretary. I'm not sure she believed what I told her, she was a bit shocked, but I gathered that a Mr Dane is in charge there. Presumably he's a partner or a fellow-director or something. Unfortunately he's gone to London for the day on the eight o'clock train—won't be back till this evening. I told her to contact him in London and tell him to meet you at the office at eight o'clock tonight. Unless you want him back earlier?'

'No,' said Spence. 'Not if he really is there on business. Did the girl give you details of his appointments?'

'Yes, I've got a note of them here.'

'Right, well, ring him yourself as soon as possible, just to make sure he hasn't hopped it.' Spence turned back to Dunbar. 'Well, what do you make of it? He was moved, wasn't he?'

'Oh yes, quite soon after death. Nasty wound on the back of the head. One blow only as far as I can tell at the moment. Radial fracture. . . . It's unusual that, you know, one blow. Normally people who do this sort of thing get into a frenzy and go on bashing away long after it's necessary. Good job for us they do, really—that way you get lots of blood splashed around. Goes on their clothes, you know.'

'Yes,' said Spence, 'I can imagine. But in this case there might not be much blood on the killer's clothes?'

'Might not be any.'

'I see. . . . How much strength would be required?'

'Nothing exceptional. Take a nice long swing, using both hands perhaps, anyone could do it.'

'A woman?'

'Oh yes.'

'What sort of weapon?'

'Blunt, reasonably heavy.'

'Metal or stone?'

'Couldn't say at the moment. Show me something with blood on it and I'll tell you if that was what did it.'

Spence scrambled to his feet and was about to move away when he paused. 'Oh—and just one other little thing.'

Dunbar smiled wearily. 'I thought for a minute you'd forgotten. You want to know when it happened.'

'Only in broad terms,' said Spence. 'To the nearest five minutes will do.'

'Between bedtime and two a.m.,' said Dunbar, as if that settled the matter.

'Whose bedtime?'

'My daughter's.'

'And how old is she?'

'Oh, about fifteen I think. Bursting out all over, anyway.'

Spence moved on, muttering rude words about pathologists in general and Dunbar in particular.

He spent the next few minutes examining Roger Parnell's car and the garage. He came away little the wiser, except for noticing that there was no hammer among the assortment of tools lying on a workbench in the garage. If Parnell had owned a hammer, perhaps it had been used to kill him. The question was, where was it now?

Spence looked at his watch: it was nine forty-five.

He decided to interview the milkman and the cleaner without further delay, and beckoned to Laurel to join him. 'We'll go next door,' he said, 'and start talking to people.' They began to walk down the drive.

'How do you want to handle these interviews?' Laurel asked.

'Good question,' said Spence. 'But it's quite a simple procedure basically. I talk and you listen. You also make notes of any relevant times, dates, figures and so on. Just the important ones, I don't want a shorthand note of the whole proceedings. Then every evening I dictate on to tape my own recollection of what people said to us, and as often as not I send someone round to take a statement from them as well. So one way and another we have quite a lot of documentation. Clear?'

'Yes, I think so,' said Laurel.

'Good,' said Spence. 'Now let's see how it works in practice.'

5

Spence and Laurel went next door and rang the front door bell. The doctor's wife, Mrs Thomson, opened the door and seemed none too pleased to see them. She was a slim blonde in her late thirties, wearing a cream blouse and brown slacks. Judging by her bad-tempered expression she obviously felt it was very inconsiderate of the murderer not to have committed his crime somewhere else.

'It would have been better if you'd come round to the back door, actually,' she said. 'The milkman and the cleaning lady are in the kitchen.'

'Oh,' said Spence, not in the least put out. 'Well, I'll have a word with them in a minute. But perhaps we could ask you a few questions first.'

'Questions?' said Mrs Thomson sharply. 'What sort of questions?'

Spence moved past her into the hall and nodded towards a half-opened door. 'Perhaps we could sit down in there?'

Mrs Thomson sighed; the day was clearly ruined beyond repair. 'Oh, very well.' She made her way into the living-room, and Spence, with a wink at his colleague, motioned to Laurel to follow her in. They all sat down on extremely elegant chairs which were upholstered in what appeared to be red velvet; their feet almost disappeared into the pile of the carpet.

'Have you any children, Mrs Thomson?' asked Spence, thinking that if she had they were surely never allowed in this spotless room.

'Oh yes. Two.'

'And where are they now?'

'I sent them down into the town. Gave them some money for the amusement arcades. It's not something I would encourage normally, of course, but in the circumstances . . .' She smiled bravely.

'Yes,' said Spence. 'They're best out of it. . . . Mrs Thomson, how well did you know Roger Parnell?'

Mrs Thomson squirmed visibly. 'Only very slightly. We've only been here six months. We've lived in the town for some years, of course, but we've only recently moved into the Avenue.'

'I see. So after you moved in I suppose you introduced yourselves.'

'Well, not quite. I didn't meet Mr Parnell for some weeks, actually. But then I noticed that he had a cleaning woman, Mrs Meadows, who came to him three days a week, so I went round to see if she could also work for me.'

'And could she?'

'Yes, she used to do Roger on Monday, Wednesday and Friday mornings, and she came to me on the other two days. It's not as much as I'd like of course, but it's difficult to get reliable people these days.'

'You're so right,' said Spence. 'You're so right. . . . What sort of man was he?'

Mrs Thomson's eyes wandered over to a massive Canaletto reproduction on the wall; it had a gilt frame three inches wide. 'Well,' she said slowly, 'he was . . . young. Well off, I should say.'

'Popular?'

'He was quite well known in the district.'

'But not popular.'

'Oh he was liked well enough. It was just that he was—well, in my youth we would have called him NSIT.'

'Not safe in taxis?'

'Precisely.'

'Made a pass at you, did he?' said Spence thoughtfully.

'That's rather a vulgar way of putting it.'

'But nevertheless that's what he did. Tried to put his hand up your skirt.'

Mrs Thomson went rather pale. 'I had to tell him to keep his hands to himself,' she said primly. 'I'd prefer not to say where he put them.'

The phone rang, temporarily relieving Mrs Thomson's embarrassment. She picked up the receiver.

'Hello?' She listened for a few moments. 'I think I'd better hand you over to the policeman,' she said. 'Just hold on.' She held out the receiver for Spence, her hand over the mouthpiece. 'It's Tina White,' she said in a whisper.

'Should I know the lady?' asked Spence.

'She's the wife of our local MP,' said Mrs Thomson, as if anyone but a congenital idiot would have known that without being told. Spence took the telephone without comment.

'Detective Superintendent Spence here,' he said. 'Can I help you, Mrs White?'

'I've heard a rumour.' The voice at the other end

spoke very clearly and carefully. 'A rumour that Roger Parnell has been murdered. Can you confirm or deny it, please?'

'I can confirm it,' said Spence.

There was a pause and then the line went dead. Spence put the receiver back on its rest. 'Goodbye, Mrs White,' he said. He returned his attention to the doctor's wife. 'Mrs White also knew Mr Parnell, I take it?'

'I really couldn't say,' said Mrs Thomson, her chin in the air.

'I don't like to be deliberately misled, Mrs. Thomson,' said Spence. 'Did she to your knowledge know Roger Parnell, or didn't she?'

Mrs Thomson was rattled. 'Well, of course she knew him.' An edge of hysteria crept into her voice. 'Of course she knew him. She only lives just up the road, we all know each other.' She took a handkerchief out of her sleeve and blew her nose fiercely.

Spence had had enough of Mrs Thomson, for the time being at any rate. He stood up. 'Well, thank you very much for your help. I'll just have a word with the people in the kitchen and then we'll be off. No need for you to come with us.'

6

The milkman, one Albert Jenkins, and the cleaning
lady, Mrs Meadows, were sitting over a pot of tea at
the kitchen table. One of Laurel's men had already
interviewed them, and Spence glanced quickly through
their written statements as he sat at the table beside
them; all the important points seemed to have been
covered.

Albert Jenkins was a small, nervous-looking individual of about thirty-five. He wore a white, knee-
length coat with black trousers beneath it; his white
peaked cap lay on the table beside him.

'So you came up the drive,' said Spence, 'turned him
over to see what the trouble was—'

'Oh no,' said Jenkins firmly. 'I didn't turn him over.
I never touched him.'

'I think you must have done,' said Spence. 'He was
lying on his front as you came up the drive, and you
turned him over to see who it was.'

'No!' said Jenkins. Spence had him worried. 'I
could see his face as soon as I come in the drive. I
knew who it was all the time, I've seen him every
Saturday for years when he paid me. . . . I thought
he was drunk at first, and then when I got closer I
could see all the blood. Even then I didn't think about

murder. I mean you don't, do you? I just thought he'd
had a nasty accident, hit his head on the doorstep or
something. So I went and got the doctor.'

'All right. So you didn't move him. I accept that.
But did you move anything else?'

'How do you mean?'

'Well, was there anything else beside the body? A
stone, a metal bar, anything like that?'

'No, nothing. I never touched nothing. I didn't like
the look of him, if you really want to know. I went
back down the drive, shooed the paper boy away, and
then come round here.'

'All right.' Spence was satisfied. 'That's all, Mr Jenkins. You can go now.'

Albert Jenkins could hardly believe his ears. He
had had one or two previous brushes with the law—a
misunderstanding over some ladies' underwear, for
instance—and the interviews on those occasions had
lasted very much longer. It was with some relief that
he went back to finish his milk round.

Spence turned his attention to Mrs Meadows, who
seemed likely to be a much richer source of information than either Mrs Thomson or the milkman.

Mrs Meadows was fiftyish, and decidedly short and
stout; Spence guessed that after any exertion she would
become very short of breath. Her brown hair was
tightly curled, close to her head, as if she had recently
had a very cheap perm. Her face was pale and drawn,
the eyes frightened and large behind thick lenses in
colourless plastic frames. Her sex appeal was zero. She
was wearing an ancient brown overcoat with the top
button dangling loose; she fingered it anxiously,
doubtless wishing she had taken the trouble to sew
it on properly. Under the coat Spence could see a light-

blue nylon overall. Beside her, on the floor, was a large green shopping bag.

'Now then, Mrs Meadows,' said Spence. 'I'd like to ask you a few questions. It won't take long, and then I'll get you taken home so that you can put your feet up a bit. I expect it's all been a bit of a shock.'

'Yes, sir,' said Mrs Meadows. 'It has.'

'All right. . . . Now, how long have you been working for Mr Parnell?'

'Fifteen years. Well, not for Mr Parnell all that time, of course. I mean he was only a boy in the beginning. But for the family, fifteen years.'

'They lived here all that time?'

'Yes, sir.'

'And what did Mr Parnell's father do?'

'He was an architect. A very good one, so I understand. He died about two years after I started. Roger would be about thirteen then. His birthday's in the summer, June the fourth.'

'So he'd be . . . twenty-six this year?'

'Yes, that's right. . . .' Mrs Meadows reflected. 'It doesn't seem fair, does it? Getting killed when you're twenty-six. But nearly all that family's gone now. All of them.'

She seemed about to have a little weep, so Spence moved on rapidly.

'What about Mrs Parnell—is she alive?'

'Oh no, sir. She died four years ago. Just about this time it was, just before Christmas. Quite sudden, not like her husband. Heart, you know. Roger was away at the time, working in London. But then when his mother passed on he decided to come back here and live in the house. I was surprised he did, really.'

'Why?'

'Well, it was too big for one thing, too big for a bachelor. He liked it though, liked the whole of this area, that's why he came back.'

'And you cleaned the place up for him three days a week, I gather.'

'Yes, that's right. He trusted me to see to it, gave me my own key and everything. I know that house as well as I know my own.'

'Did he have any brothers and sisters?'

'One brother, one sister. His brother was in the army, doing very well. He was an officer of course. But then he was killed in Northern Ireland, five years ago. Broke his mother's heart, that did. She faded a lot after that, I always thought.'

'And what about the sister?'

'She's married. Gone to America. Married an Englishman, mind you, but she's over in America somewhere. I should be able to tell you the address, I've been sitting here trying to remember it because I know you'll want to get in touch with her. But it's gone. It'll be over there in the house somewhere. There are letters and things.'

'Are there any other relatives that you know of?'

'Well . . . Roger has an uncle in Birmingham somewhere. I don't know much about him, they didn't have much to do with him. Mrs. Parnell used to say that there was some trouble about money years ago, but I'm not sure even she knew what it was all about. He was Mr Parnell's brother, you see.'

'Yes,' said Spence, 'I understand.' He lifted the lid of the teapot and found it was still half full; he topped up Mrs Meadows's cup. 'I don't know whether this is worth drinking, but let's try it anyway.'

'Thank you, sir. That's very kind.'

Spence waited until she had stirred two spoonfuls of sugar into the cup and drunk half of it, and then went on. 'So you knew Roger most of his life?'

'Yes, I suppose I did. Watched him grow up.'

'Went away to school, did he?'

'When he was thirteen, yes. Went to Tallmead. That's one of the top ten, so they say.'

'University?'

'Manchester. Till he was twenty-one. Then he went to London. Got a job in a sort of bank I believe it was. His mother did explain it to me but I didn't understand the details of it. He changed his job after a while, still in London, but then when his mother died he came back here.'

'And what did he do when he did come back?'

'Well, he started a business of his own, you know. Southey and Moore, that's his firm, down in the town. Insurance brokers. Of course he didn't actually start it, he just took it over. The firm's been there for some time.'

'I suppose his mother left him enough money to do that?'

'Yes, the house and about thirty thousand pounds. That's no secret, it was in the paper. She left it all to him because Catherine, that's Roger's sister, her husband is a quite a rich man I believe. But Roger never kept any cash in the house, not more than a few pounds anyway, so whoever it was that killed him was wasting their time. Bashed on the head from behind, wasn't he?'

'I'm afraid he was, yes.'

Mrs Meadows shook her head. 'Dirty trick, that. But

they'd have to do it that way because he could look
after himself, could Roger. He was a boxer, you know,
won a lot of medals at school.'

'I'm interested to hear that he was his own boss,' –
said Spence. 'He could choose his own working hours,
I suppose—suit himself?'

'Well, yes, more or less. But he had a partner, you
know. Mr White.'

'Our friend the local MP?'

'Yes, sir, that's right. He lives just up the road, and
he and Roger's dad were big pals years ago. He put
up part of the money and Roger put up the rest. But
Mr White didn't do any of the actual work, he left all
that to Roger.'

'I see. . . . Now then, if I read you correctly, Mrs
Meadows, you're very upset about Mr Parnell's death.'

'I am, sir. I am that.'

'And you'd like to help catch the person who killed
him.' Mrs Meadows nodded, gnawing her lower lip.
'All right. Now if you're going to help me—really help
me—you've got to tell me the truth. Not what you'd
like to have been true. Not what you think you
ought to say, just because Roger's dead. But the truth
—what really happened, what people were really like.
OK?'

'Yes, sir.'

'Fine. Now then—did Mr Parnell treat you fairly?'

'Oh yes. Very fair.'

'He never got angry?'

'No.'

'And he paid you regularly.'

'Oh yes. And with a good grace. Which is more
than I can say for some.' Mrs Meadows nodded towards the door to the hall.

'Was he popular with the neighbours?'

A hesitation.

'The truth, now,' Spence prompted her.

'Well—not popular. I wouldn't say that. They liked him, you know. Most of them anyway. But I think they were a little bit frightened of him.'

'Why?'

'I don't know. Unless it was because he was young, and fancy free, and had a fair bit of money in his pocket.'

'Did he have any enemies, people who would want to kill him?'

'Not that would want to kill him, not as far as I know.'

'But he had enemies.'

Mrs. Meadows looked down at her hands. 'I suppose he did, if the truth be known. He got into trouble as a boy—but then all lads do.'

'What sort of trouble?'

'What do you think?'

'Girls.'

Mrs Meadows nodded. 'As long as I've known him, really. He was a lively lad, even when he was thirteen. If I had a pound for every girl he's been out with I wouldn't need to clean for other people any more, that's certain.'

'They tell me that there's a girls' school at the bottom of his garden—Petal Park School. Was there trouble there?'

'Oh yes, sir, all the time. They say you shouldn't speak ill of the dead, but it's true. His sister used to go there, so of course . . . His mother used to weep about it, but I used to say it's only natural, isn't it? A boy like that, with a couple of hundred girls just over the fence, and no father to keep him in line—of course he was going to be interested. And people did say some hard things over the years—very hard things. But it takes two to tango, that's what I always say.'

'What about after his mother died? Did he still go on seeing girls from the school?'

'Well, not just girls from the school, sir. He had plenty of other girl friends as well. But the Petal Park girls did use to come over from time to time, that's a fact. I used to find lipstick and powder and such—' For the first time the ghost of a smile flitted across Mrs Meadows's face. 'So I knew what was going on all right.'

'And how did the school feel about this?'

Mrs Meadows shrugged. 'Oh, well. They made a mountain out of a molehill in my opinion. Occasionally there was a fuss. Particularly one time—one of the teachers came over, Miss Leigh her name is, she's in charge of the boarders.'

'Ah yes,' said Spence. 'I met her a few minutes ago, walking her dog. She used to object, did she?'

'Oh yes, sir. This one time in particular she had a row with Roger outside his back door, and somehow or other she pushed him and a window got broken. Roger cut his elbow and had a couple of stitches in it. And the next thing I heard, the story was all over the district that Miss Leigh had come round to the house and smashed all the windows, in a fit of temper. Which wasn't true. It was an accident. And only one window got broken.'

'When was this?'

'Oh, the summer before last. But it was a storm in a teacup and it all blew over. Miss Brockway, she's the headmistress, she came over and apologized. And then she sent her caretaker over to mend the window, Mr Gray. So it was all forgotten in no time.'

'But not by the neighbours.'

'Oh no, they talked about it for months. But not to me—I wouldn't listen.'

'Did he get into any fights, young Roger? Outside the boxing ring, I mean.'

'No, none that I ever heard of. But if he had, he'd have taken good care of himself. Like I told you, see, he was a boxer. No, the only way anyone could get the best of him would be in the dark. Come at him in the dark, from behind, and bash him over the head. Whoever did that was a bastard, that's what I say.'

The tea had gone cold and Spence felt that he had got as much out of Mrs Meadows as he could; he asked Laurel to see that she was taken home in a police car. He himself jotted down a few notes and left the house shortly afterwards, thanking Mrs Thomson warmly for allowing him to conduct the interviews in her kitchen.

'You're welcome,' said Mrs Thomson. But her smile was unconvincing.

7

It was half past ten when Spence came away from the doctor's house. Next door the men from the mobile forensic laboratory were just finishing their work and an ambulance crew were waiting for permission to remove the body.

Before he gave that permission Spence knelt down on the cold drive and went through Roger Parnell's pockets. There was nothing unusual in them but the contents were all listed carefully and dispatched to Detective Sergeant Wilberforce to be placed in store.

Having first made sure that they had been fingerprinted, Spence then picked up the bunch of keys which were lying beside the empty milk bottles; he used the obvious one to let himself and Laurel into Parnell's house. The body of Roger Parnell was then removed from the drive and everyone else departed—all except one uniformed constable, who remained at the gate to discourage sightseers for the rest of the day.

'We'll start at the top of the house and work down,' said Spence as he and Laurel climbed the stairs. 'Don't touch anything more than you have to—we'll get the fingerprint boys in here this afternoon. We'll get the loft searched as well, including under the insulation, if there is any.'

They reached the landing. 'Now then,' said Spence, 'let's start in here.' He opened a door. 'Hmm. Main bedroom by the look of it. One double bed, not been slept in, one chest of drawers with the drawers pulled out, and some clothes thrown around.'

'Either Mr Parnell was a very untidy young man,' said Laurel, 'or else whoever broke that window on the ground floor also ransacked the place.'

'Looks like it,' said Spence. 'We shall see. Let's have a look in the wardrobe.' He crossed to a large built-in unit with louvre doors and opened them to reveal a row of suits. 'Well, no surprises here—obviously this was Parnell's bedroom. . . . OK, let's move on.'

The next room was another bedroom containing two single beds; nothing in it had been disturbed and it looked as if it was seldom used.

The room adjoining was in total darkness and Spence had to grope around for a light-switch, which he eventually discovered was operated by a cord from the ceiling.

'Ah. A dark-room. Must have been very keen on photography, Mr Parnell. Not many people bother to equip themselves with a proper dark-room in their own home.'

'But then he did have the space for it,' said Laurel. 'And then some. A big house this, for a bachelor.'

They stepped inside the dark-room and looked around. Laid out on a bench were Parnell's cameras, four of them, of varying film sizes; one had a motor drive attachment, and there was an assortment of interchangeable lenses, including a huge Russian tele-

photo. There was also an eight-millimetre film pro-
jector.

Spence pointed to the telephoto lens. 'What do
you think he wanted this for?' he asked.

'Well, perhaps he was interested in photographing
Mother Nature,' said Laurel. 'Animals, or birds maybe, things that would run off if he went too close to
them.'

'What a nice man you are,' said Spence. 'I think it's
much more likely myself that he enjoyed taking photos
of people unawares. Care to bet on which it was?'

Laurel grinned. 'No, sir.'

Spence opened the door of a fourth room on the
landing, which turned out to be the bathroom. This
contained nothing more interesting than a shower with
a thermostatic control and a large selection of expensive aftershave lotions, colognes and talcs.

The last room on the landing proved to be the most
interesting. Its window looked out on to the back garden, and in the distance stood Petal Park School for
Girls.

'Bingo,' said Spence.

The room was a study. It contained a desk, a chair,
two filing cabinets and some cupboards. The drawers
of the desk and the filing cabinets were all open, as
were the doors of the cupboards; the floor was inches
deep in the paper and photographs which had been
emptied out of them.

Spence stepped carefully into the room and picked
up one of the photographs: it was of a girl, very naked,
with a saucy grin on her face; it appeared to have been
taken on the patio at the rear of the house.

'There you are,' said Spence. 'That's the kind of
nature photography Roger Parnell went in for. Nature

in the raw, you might say. . . . Judging by what we have here he never took pictures of anything else.'

'Oh, I don't know,' said Laurel. He knelt down by the door. 'There are some shots of motor racing over here. Quite professional too. Looks as if that's what he used the telephoto for.'

'Oh yes,' grunted Spence. 'I think he had other uses for it too.' He brandished a sheaf of ten by eight prints and held them up for Laurel to see. They were all rather grainy enlargements and they all featured glimpses of young ladies in various stages of undress, getting into and coming out of showers and lying on their beds in their nighties. Even the most inexperienced detective could have deduced that they were shots taken from Roger Parnell's house of the girls in Petal Park School, about a hundred yards away across the park.

Laurel whistled. 'Dirty bugger,' he said thoughtfully. 'If Miss Brockway saw those she'd go spare.'

'She's the headmistress, isn't she?'

'Yes, that's right. I met her once, when I was Fire-arms Officer—she goes in for target shooting.'

'Strait-laced, is she?' asked Spence, continuing to sort through the photographs.

'No, I wouldn't say that. Quite the opposite really. Quite racy for a girls' school headmistress. Drives an MGB.'

'Married?'

'No.'

'How old?'

'Oh, about my age.'

'Forty-seven, you mean.'

Laurel ignored him. 'Ever since our first meeting I've been trying to summon up the courage to ask her to go out with me. But checking over her guns didn't seem to be a very promising introduction somehow.'

'Oh I don't know,' said Spence. 'Anyway, we shall have to go and see her sooner or later, so she'll know you a bit better after that. . . . I don't know what she'll make of these photos. Looks as if her girls have been a bit careless in their dormitories and changing rooms.'

'Well, they are pretty isolated out there in the park,' said Laurel. 'They weren't to know that Peeping Roger was over here taking snapshots.'

'True,' said Spence. 'And of course it may have taken him years and years to bag this lot. It might be the cream of a lifetime of neck-craning. We'll get someone to log it all and bring it all down to the station this afternoon—the men can draw lots for the privilege of sorting it out. . . . Come on, let's go downstairs.'

'Just a minute,' said Laurel. 'Take a look at this.' He was examining a letter in a glass-fronted frame on the wall. ' "Dear Roger",' he quoted. ' "This is just to say that I resign. I have had enough, more than enough, of your hypocrisy, your slimy charm, and your total lack of ethics. I am fed up with being overworked, underpaid, and carrying the can for all your mistakes and idleness. In short, I have had you and your firm in a big way. Yours without regret, Alec." Who's Alec, I wonder?'

'Shouldn't be too difficult to find out,' said Spence. 'It's written on Southey and Moore notepaper, and Southey and Moore was Parnell's firm. He's listed as one of the directors.'

'Why do you think he had it framed?'

'I dunno. Probably thought it was a big joke. From what I know of him so far I can't think he hung it there as a spur to self-improvement. . . . We'll follow it up later—I'm just skimming the surface at the moment. Let's go downstairs.'

The living-room was relatively undisturbed, apart from the broken glass on the carpet and two newspapers left open on a settee. A twenty-six-inch colour television set and some elaborate hi-fi equipment were untouched.

Spence collected an address book from beside the telephone and then he and Laurel passed on into the dining-room. Here too all was neat and tidy.

The kitchen was airy, clean and spacious. A wine rack offered some bottles with expensive labels and the cupboards contained some unusual items from Fortnum and Mason in addition to the usual baked beans and rice pudding.

Off the hall was a small cloakroom, spotlessly clean, and outside the back door was an outhouse with an oil-fired central heating boiler.

'That's it, then,' said Spence when they had briefly examined every room. 'Let's go and sit down for a minute and draw breath.'

The two men moved into the living-room and relaxed in the easy chairs. It was a large room, running from front to back of the house, with windows at each end.

'Come on then,' said Spence amiably. 'Think aloud. Tell me what you make of it.'

Laurel looked around him. 'Well,' he said, 'the house must be worth about three times as much as mine, at least. It's all in good order, well decorated, rewired in the not-too-distant past. It must be hellish expensive for a single man. Can't think why he lived here.'

'Ah,' said Spence, wagging his finger. 'It's the school. The school, Mr Laurel. Just think of it. All those girls in their nighties. Parnell grew up here. He was hooked on it. Think how you would feel if you lived here. You get up in the morning, there they are getting dressed. Buy yourself a good powerful telescope and there's no knowing what you might see. And then in the afternoon they're out there again, playing hockey in their navy-blues, with thighs flashing like nobody's business. And so on.'

'All right,' said Laurel, 'so that's why he lived here. I'll accept that for the moment. But I still think it's an awfully expensive way to get your kicks. I think we ought to look into his finances.'

'We will,' said Spence, 'don't worry. But what actually happened, do you think? How did he come to get killed?'

'Well, at the moment it looks as though someone broke in, they were ransacking the place, and he disturbed them. They panicked, cracked him on the skull, and then departed.'

Spence pursed his lips. 'It's a possibility,' he said. 'It's a line we shall have to pursue. We'll have to get our ear to the ground among the local breakers and enterers. But it's not right, though, is it?'

'How do you mean, not right?'

'Well, it doesn't work. It doesn't smell right. Whoever broke in here wasn't stealing—they were searching. The place is littered with valuables—the cameras upstairs, the TV, the hi-fi, the silver in the dining-room—and none of it is gone. It's all still here.'

'That's because they were interrupted.'

'But they weren't interrupted. Parnell hadn't come come in yet. The key was in his hand, he dropped it when he was hit.'

Laurel's fingers tapped on the arm of his chair. 'It might have happened as I said, though,' he continued doggedly. 'Parnell might have come in, heard movement, and gone out again to raise the alarm.'

'And meanwhile, chummy upstairs jumped out of the bedroom window at the back, ran round to the front of the house, Parnell turned round so that his head was to the door, and then chummy hit him. Like that, you mean.'

Laurel shrugged. 'Well, of course—it sounds absurd if you put it like that.'

'Yes, it does,' said Spence, quite without malice. 'I agree. Completely absurd. But don't worry, you've probably got it right. If there's one thing that's certain about a murder case it's that anything can happen, take my word for it. The most obvious explanation is usually the wrong one. All you can do is follow up what seems to be the most likely line of inquiry, and at the same time follow up all the unlikely ones as well. So you can chase your local thieves as hard as you like—it's your patch, so you can organize that. OK?'

'OK,' said Laurel.

Spence looked at his watch. 'Eleven o'clock already. It's time we went back to base.'

8

The London Road police station was old, dark and overcrowded, which was why Spence had ordered his mobile office unit positioned on the car park at the rear. Police stations almost invariably were short of space and Spence had decided a long time ago, after his first murder case, that the simplest way of establishing a base to work from was to take your own.

The office was twenty-seven feet long, with a door in the centre; this door opened into a narrow hallway, off which two other doors opened, one to the left and one to the right, providing a room at each end.

'Come inside,' said Spence to Laurel. 'I'll show you round. . . . To the left, my office. Just a desk and a chair and a couple of other chairs, one for you if necessary. We get telephone connections, electric light and heat through cables from the station. All very cosy. . . . And at the other end of the unit, Sergeant Wilberforce's office.'

They went through the narrow door into the right-hand office and Laurel nodded to Sergeant Wilberforce.

'Wilberforce is acting as my administrative officer,' said Spence. 'Now, you and I haven't worked together on a murder case before, not as a team, anyway, but you probably know the drill as well as I do. It's Wilberforce's job to keep track of all the paperwork and to see that everything we want to have done is done. All the written records are kept in here, at least until they start to take up too much room. Whenever you think of something that needs doing, write it down straightaway on one of these job cards, before you forget it.'

Spence passed Laurel a handful of pocket-sized cards.

'They're all numbered, and every so often, when it's convenient, you hand the completed cards to Wilberforce. His job is to make sure that someone is detailed to do the work on the card, to check that we get a written report when it is done, and to check that you and I both read it. When we have read it, it goes on file, it's indexed and cross-referenced. OK?'

Laurel nodded.

'Fine. Now the first few jobs are obvious.' Spence began to scribble. 'Search Parnell's house and bring back here all photographs and films and written documents generally. . . . Sort and list them. . . . Photograph the house in its present state first. . . . Fingerprint it. . . . Search the garden, looking in particular for any signs of vomit or faeces—murderers often get a bit loose at one end or the other. . . . Go through victim's wallet and check on credit cards, club membership, etc. . . . Institute door-to-door inquiries. . . . Inform next of kin—details in victim's address book. And so on. And already we've got more than enough job cards to keep us and our men occupied for the rest of the day. . . . Now, what I want you to do now is give Sergeant Wilberforce a list of the twenty men you've got lined up to help us, their strengths and their weaknesses, local knowledge and so forth. That way he can allocate the right jobs to the right people. For instance, on the door-to-door inquiries we want the two most able men to go and see that girl who drove up to the house this morning, Dawn Stenning. And the same pair to call at the MP's house, the White household. We'll see all those people ourselves later on, but not immediately. In fact that's the usual pattern, two sets of interviews with all the important people. If you and I see them first, we send a couple of men along afterwards, just to see if they tell the same story. And if the door-to-door men get there first, you and I study their statement to see if we can knock any holes in it.'

'And no doubt these double visits are going to annoy people just as much as usual,' said Laurel.

'No doubt,' said Spence. 'But we aren't in business to make people happy, we're here to solve a murder. Now, what time have you arranged this briefing?'

'Twelve noon, over in the station.'

'OK. Well, you list the names and the other details for Sergeant Wilberforce, and I'll just report the state of play and collect my thoughts.'

Spence went into his own end of the mobile office unit and phoned the Assistant Chief Constable (Crime). The latter was a remote figure more often found on the Wellbridge golf course than at the scene of murder investigations, but a man who had to be kept informed. Spence gave him a summary of the events so far.

'Hmm, well, sounds all right,' said the ACC. 'Pity that Booth is laid up, though. Got a lot of experience, has Booth.'

'Yes, sir,' said Spence, acknowledging the truth of the statement but wishing that the ACC could have sounded a little more confident in his own abilities.

'Can I be of any help at all?' the ACC continued.

'I think we're all right for manpower at the moment, sir,' said Spence as neutrally as possible, and he was relieved when the offer of assistance was not pressed home.

Spence put the phone down and began to prepare some notes on what he wanted to say at the forthcoming briefing, but after a few minutes Sergeant Wilberforce knocked on the office door and announced the arrival of the press and a television crew. Fortunately Wilberforce had already prepared a brief written statement and had cleared it with headquarters, so Spence had something ready to hand out to the local reporters. He also gave a short filmed interview in the station yard, having first satisfied himself that Wilberforce was on the phone to the next of kin, in the shape of Parnell's uncle in Birmingham. No mention was made, either in the handout or in the interview, of the broken window at the rear of the house and the disturbance upstairs.

At twelve o'clock the briefing session was held in a bare, dusty room in the London Road police station. Twenty members of the CID, plus one Woman Detective Sergeant and two Women Detective Constables, listened with close attention as Spence described what he wanted them to do. As he spoke Spence wondered to what extent their concentration was sharpened by a desire to get the whole thing settled by Christmas, now only three days away. That was bound to act as an incentive. And if the murder hunt was still on come Christmas day, a lot of wives were going to feel very cross indeed.

'Everything depends on detail,' Spence told them in

summary. 'Get the small details right and the whole picture begins to make sense. This afternoon it's house-to-house inquiries in teams of two. Find out if anyone saw anything unusual—parked cars, strangers in the district, people not being where they usually are at a particular time. Get people to talk to you and then get it all down on paper so that I can see what you've learnt. . . . It's twelve-thirty now—grab something to eat and then get on with it.'

There was a general scraping of feet and rattling of chairs and the room emptied rapidly.

'We have to eat too,' Spence told Laurel. 'It's a mistake not to.' So they followed the men to the canteen.

Over lunch Spence steered the conversation round to Laurel's family. 'How old are your kids now?' he asked. 'Twelve or so?'

'Fifteen and thirteen,' said Laurel. 'And they're fairly self-sufficient. I'm quite lucky really, there's a neighbour who keeps an eye on them if I'm home late in the evenings, and they'll be OK tonight for instance.'

'Good,' said Spence. 'I don't know what we'll be doing tonight but I don't suppose it'll be watching telly with our feet up. We could be in a pub finding out if anyone knows anything about this break-in. That's a thought. Do a job card—check the cleaning lady's family for criminal connections. Mrs. Meadows was the name, Ruth Meadows. Can you think of anything else?'

'Not at the moment,' said Laurel.

'All right. Dinner settled OK?'

'I think so.'

'Good. In that case we'll go to the post mortem.'

9

Dr Dunbar had made arrangements for the body of Roger Parnell to be taken to the mortuary of the hospital in Shireport. While they were on their way there Spence explained to Laurel why they were bothering to go at all.

'Occasionally you don't learn anything,' he said. 'But that's the exception. Usually you learn a great deal—about the victim, about how he lived, and how he died. But most of all, going to the post-mortem brings it home to you that this person really is dead, and that it's up to you to find the murderer, as fast as you possibly can. That's why I go—it gives me an incentive to work harder.'

The mortuary, like most of its kind, was a gloomy little building which outwardly resembled a public lavatory. The interior continued the same theme, with large areas of white tile and a smell of disinfectant; the fluorescent lights ruthlessly highlighted the ugliness of the place.

It was two o'clock when Spence and Laurel arrived, and Dr Dunbar was already dressed for action. He was wearing a red rubber apron over a green smock, with a green cap fitting tightly over his bald head;

apart from a pair of gym shoes he did not appear to be wearing anything else.

Roger Parnell's body was lying naked under the lights, his head supported by a block of wood. The clothes had been carefully removed and sealed in polythene bags for detailed examination later.

'Interesting fellow,' said Dr Dunbar thoughtfully, as he dictated notes on the state of the body to his assistant. 'He was wearing pink women's knickers for underpants. I think I shall had to try that some time, they looked quite comfortable. . . . The body, you will observe, was moved after death. Turned over from lying on its front to lying on its back. You see these marks?'

'Lividity,' said Spence.

'Exactly. In my opinion he was moved between half an hour and an hour after death.' The way Dunbar said it suggested that his opinion was authoritative.

Pausing only to tell an extremely dirty story about a Chinese policeman, Dunbar then seized a scalpel and opened up the body in one long incision from the throat to the symphysis pubis. A police photographer recorded the operation on videotape, just in case anyone ever needed to see it again.

Spence was used to the procedure these days and only when Dunbar came to work on the head did he feel at all squeamish. The scalp was slit right across the top and rolled back grotesquely in both directions, leaving the skull exposed. Then, with a surgical saw, Dunbar removed the top of the head to examine the brain. By that point the body had become a mere shell, only a distant memory of a human being called Roger Parnell.

'Well,' said Spence eventually, 'would you like to express an opinion as to the cause of death?'

Dunbar looked up from his work. 'Someone conked him on the head, didn't they?' he said. And, until they received his written report, that was all they could get out of him.

10

By three forty-five p.m. Spence and Laurel were both
back in Spence's half of the mobile office unit. They
drank tea provided by Percy Wilberforce and looked
through a large carton of eight-millimetre films, colour
slides, and black-and-white prints; all these had been
brought in by the men searching Parnell's house.

'I suppose these commercial eight-millimetres will
have to be looked at by somebody,' said Spence. 'I
don't suppose they're relevant—they're all the sort of
soft porn you can buy down on Shireport promenade.
But you never know, there might just be a face that
someone recognizes. Being the sort of man he was,
Parnell may even have dabbled in the blue movie
business himself in some way. He certainly seems to
have had plenty of spare cash.'

'Well I'm damned!' said Laurel, who was sorting
through the black-and-white prints.

'What's that?'

Laurel held up a print for Spence to see. 'A shot of
Miss Brockway in the nude. Taken without her knowledge, of course, through the telephoto lens. But there
she is, large as life, just getting out of a shower.'

Spence examined it. 'Hmm. The grain on it is enormous—he must have enlarged these things about seven

hundred times. Looks as if it was taken through a window of the girls' changing room after a game of hockey or something—there seem to be some clothes hanging up in the background. . . . She's a handsome woman anyway—wasted without a man in her life. . . . What are the others like?'

'A mixture,' said Laurel. 'They fall into two categories—shots of the girls of Petal Park, taken from a great distance, with very small parts of the negative enlarged to enormous proportions to reveal the odd tit or bum. The trouble that man would take for a shot of a piece of flesh is amazing. And then there are another variety.' He held up a sample. 'These are all shots of girls who were obviously very willing posers indeed. In fact by the look of it most of them revelled in it.'

Spence grunted. 'Do a job card then and get copies made of the faces of all the willing ones and show them around. See if any of your men can recognize the girls involved. But only the faces, mind. We don't want any leering, or the girls could quite reasonably complain. They posed for Parnell's benefit, not for ours. Split the prints into the two categories you mentioned and put them in two separate folders. . . . Now—do you see any sort of motive in any of this?'

'You mean a motive for killing Parnell?'

'Yes.'

'Not at the moment. You can read a motive into it, of course, and God knows, wherever you get attractive girls taking their clothes off you get trouble. People get jealous and so on. So you can always conceive of a motive.'

'For instance.'

'Well, Parnell seduced someone's sister, or fiancée.

The bloke didn't like it and decided to settle his hash.'

'Or?'

'Or—Parnell gave one of the girls a copy of one of these photographs, and her dad found it. And he got mad and bashed him. And so on.'

'Ad nauseam.' said Spence. 'I'm afraid you're right. Anyway, bring those photos with you, both categories, and we'll go round to Petal Park School and see if Miss Brockway had any idea what was going on. I don't somehow think she'll be very pleased.'

11

Soon afterwards Laurel drove his green Ford Escort 1100L up the London Road to Petal Park School, with Spence in the front passenger seat. It was dusk now and most cars were driving on their sidelights.

'We'll follow the same drill as this morning,' said Spence. 'I ask the questions and for the most part you just sit there and observe. If your local knowledge is relevant you can catch my eye and chip in, but generally speaking what I want you to do is watch the reactions so that I can compare notes with you afterwards.'

'OK,' said Laurel. He turned the car off the London Road and up the long sweeping drive which led to the school. On the left, at the entrance to the drive, was a small detached house: lights were on in the ground-floor rooms.

'That must be The Lodge,' said Spence.

'It is,' Laurel confirmed.

'Where Dawn Stenning lives. . . . Not a bad address, that—the Lodge, Petal Park. I wonder what her husband does.'

On either side of the drive as they proceeded up it were playing fields, and then Petal Park School itself began to loom up out of the darkness ahead, with lights shining at random in its silhouette. The house was perhaps a hundred and fifty years old, Spence estimated, and at the wings were those familiar sights in almost every school nowadays, mobile classrooms. Can't be short of customers, thought Spence.

The two men went up the steps to the front door and rang the bell, and after a few moments the door was opened by the woman they had met walking her dog earlier in the day.

'Ah,' said Spence, 'Miss Leigh, I believe.'

'Yes, that's right. Oh—and you're the police officers, aren't you?'

'Yes,' said Spence. 'We met this morning.' He introduced himself and his colleague. 'Well now, Miss Leigh, as you may have gathered, what we're investigating is not just a mere break-in but a murder.'

'Oh yes,' said Miss Leigh. 'Yes, I heard all about it at the post office. Quite a sensation.'

'I wonder if we might come inside, and ask you a few questions?'

'About the murder?'

'Yes.'

'Well, yes, I suppose so. Although I'm bound to say I don't know how I can help you.' Miss Leigh stepped to one side and the two men entered the house. 'Ah, just a moment—here's the paper boy.' She reached out to take an evening paper from a boy who had just arrived on a bicycle; she tucked it under her arm and then closed the door. 'Will it take long, do you think?'

'Ten minutes, perhaps.'

'Oh. Well, in that case we'd better go up to the library. We've been doing the end-of-term stocktake so we've had a fire in there all day. It's the warmest room in the house at the moment.' She began to lead the way up the broad staircase.

'Where's Goldie?' said Spence. 'Out the back, I suppose.'

Miss Leigh laughed. 'Yes, indeed,' she said. 'I won't have him indoors, the girls would spoil him to death.'

She opened a heavy door at the top of the stairs and showed them into the library, a large, tall-ceilinged room lined with bookshelves made of what Spence took to be oak. Inside the room was a slim, bespectacled young man wearing a black corduroy jacket and grey trousers.

'I think we'd better call it a day now, Peter,' said Miss Leigh. 'I want to have a word with these gentlemen.' She put the evening paper into a cupboard by the door.

The young man called Peter said nothing. He just smiled politely, put down the book he had been looking at, and glided silently past the two detectives with hardly a glance at them.

'It was burglars, wasn't it?' said Miss Leigh, once they were all comfortably seated round the open fire. 'Parnell disturbed some thieves ransacking the house and got coshed. That's what Mrs Adams in the post office said, and she's usually very well informed.'

Spence didn't comment; he just smiled at Miss Leigh and recorded every detail about her in his memory. She was of average height but underweight: ectomorphic, his wife would have called her; her wrists were particularly thin. She had short, straight hair, dark brown in colour, and equally dark brown eyes which were never still. On her face there were faint traces of lipstick and powder, but they appeared to have been placed there out of a wish to conform with custom rather than out of a desire to make herself more attractive.

She was wearing a tweed skirt, a yellow blouse buttoned modestly up to the neck, and a green cardigan with brown buttons; the cardigan bore all the earmarks of having been knitted by a maiden aunt from a pattern in *Woman's Weekly*.

'We're going round to see all the local people,' said Spence by way of explanation. 'It's the usual procedure in a case like this. You probably think you've seen and heard nothing that's relevant, but you'd be surprised—the police get lots of little pieces of information which mean nothing on their own, but put together they can be very useful. . . . Now—I wonder if you could begin by telling me something about the school.'

'The school?'

'Yes.'

'Well, as you say, Superintendent, I wouldn't have thought that was relevant, but what did you want to know in particular?'

'How long has it been here, for instance?'

Miss Leigh's eyes stopped wandering from face to face and settled on a distant corner of the room. 'Well, it was established about forty years ago, more or less, by two sisters. They ran it until about five years ago, when it became an educational trust, with governors and so forth.'

'And Miss Brockway was appointed headmistresss then?'

'She was, yes.'

'Was she teaching at the school before that?'

'No. No, she was a housemistress at Farmdale, near Woking.'

'I see. And how long have you been here, Miss Leigh?'

'Eight years, just over.'

'And you've been the housemistress all that time?'

'Yes.'

And so you were passed over for the job of head-mistress, thought Spence, but he didn't say so out loud. Instead he asked: 'How many girls are there in the school?'

'About two hundred and fifty at the moment, forty of them boarders. They all broke up last Friday, of course. The place is a bit more peaceful now.'

'And what's the age range of your girls?'

'Eleven to eighteen.'

'But they thin out a bit towards the top, I imagine?'

'Oh yes. Only a minority stay on till they're eighteen. We can't cope with sixth-form work in science, not many girls' schools can these days. So quite a lot of the able girls either go off to the local tech. or to Longmere—that's a boys' public school about ten miles away.'

'Yes,' said Spence, 'I know it. How many staff do you have?'

'About fifteen, if you include part-timers.'

'And how many of those live in?'

'Only myself and Bee—Miss Brockway that is. The matron lives in during term-time but she goes away for the holidays.'

'What about the cooks and the maids?'

'They're all local. We recruit from the council estate on the other side of the London Road. . . . Forgive me, Superintendent, but I'm at a loss to know why you're asking all these questions when Mr Parnell is alleged to have been clubbed to death by a burglar.'

'Well, that's one possible explanation, Miss Leigh,' said Spence with a friendly smile. 'But there are others. And in a case like this we like to have a lot of background information. Now, to get a bit more specific, tell me about yourself and Miss Brockway. What were you doing yesterday evening?'

'Well, Miss Brockway went out to dinner and I stayed in. I read for a bit, watched television, and then I took the dog for a walk.'

'What time?'

'Oh, about half past nine.'

'And where did you go?'

'Well, down the London Road for half a mile or so and then back. I vary my route from time to time or it gets boring. After I got back I had a bath and then went to bed.'

'You were alone all evening?'

'Well, yes, I'm afraid I was.' Miss Leigh put her hand to her throat and began to fiddle with a button of her blouse. 'It's not an unusual situation,' she said, and then immediately looked as if she wished she had said nothing. She stood up, crossed to a table and returned with a box of matches and a pack of cigarettes. She lit a cigarette and then threw the match into the fire.

'Tell me about Roger Parnell,' said Spence. 'You knew him, I believe.'

'By sight, yes.'

'What can you tell me about him?'

'Not much, except that he was a confounded nuisance to the school. He had a sister who was here some years ago. It was before I came here, thank goodness, but I gather there was trouble even then.'

'What sort of trouble?'

'Well, his sister was older than he was but I understand he was precocious. I don't think I want to say more about it than that.'

'And there's been trouble more recently,' said Spence. 'In the last four years, since he came back from London.'

Miss Leigh inhaled deeply and tapped the ash into the fire before answering; she sat with her legs pressed together, hunched up, with her elbows on her knees. 'I don't know who could have told you that,' she said.

'Never mind who told me—is it true?'

Miss Leigh looked at him coldly. 'Is it really necessary to speak ill of the dead?' she asked.

'Whoever killed him might possibly kill someone else. I want to prevent that. And to catch Roger Parnell's murderer I need to know what sort of man he was.'

Miss Leigh sighed. 'Well, if you put it like that, I see your point. What sort of man was he? Well, a singularly horrible one, if you want my opinion. A slimy Peeping Tom.'

'You mean he peered through the windows?'

'No, not that quite, though I wouldn't put it past him. . . . You know, Superintendent, I try to keep an open mind, I know that times are changing and I try to be open and frank with my girls. But all I can say is that for a grown man to go leching after teenage girls is just about as low as you can get.'

'But if he didn't peep through windows then what did he do exactly?'

Miss Leigh straightened up and spoke with sharp

disapproval. 'He used to come and watch hockey and netball matches, that sort of thing. It was all very awkward. He used to know lots of parents and lots of the older girls, and he was a very good mixer. He could be very charming if he wished. And, of course, he was a friend of the chairman of our governors. That made life very difficult indeed.'

'Oh?' said Spence. 'And who is your chairman?'

'Marcus White,' said Miss Leigh. 'The local MP. He lives—'

'Just down the road,' said Spence. 'Yes, I know. Tell me, did you have any trouble with your boarders—girls sneaking over to Parnell's house after hours?'

'I did,' said Miss Leigh grimly. 'It was open house over there. They could go any time, day or night. Drink his sherry, smoke his cigarettes and listen to all the latest pop records. . . . Needless to say it was absolutely forbidden of course, and most of them had more sense, but there were always one or two. Those who wanted to look big, or were feeling disgruntled and wanted someone to grumble to. I was very rarely able to catch any of them red-handed, I may say, but I knew what went on. I have my sources of information.'

Just like the KGB, thought Spence.

At that moment there was the sound of a car drawing up outside.

'Ah,' said Miss Leigh, 'I think that sounds like Miss Brockway.' She went to the window and looked out. 'Yes, it is. I'll just go and tell her you're here.'

12

Miss Leigh went out on to the landing and Spence followed her. She leaned over the stout wooden rail and looked down into the hall below. 'Bee?' she called.

'Hello,' said a cheerful voice, and a moment later Miss Brockway began to climb the stairs.

Spence recognized her at once. The photograph of her which was currently lying in a folder on Laurel's lap was grainy and indistinct, but quite unmistakable. She was a tall, handsome woman with a well-proportioned figure. Spence guessed that she was nearing forty, but she carried her years well. She had black hair which was drawn into a bun at the back of her head, but it was a stylish bun, not a prim and prissy one. The eyes were very dark and piercing, and the lines around her mouth suggested that she often smiled. Her cheeks were slightly flushed, and her clothes confirmed the impression that she had spent the afternoon out in the open air. She was wearing a gold roll-neck sweater and a brown suede safari jacket over a dark-green pleated skirt; her strongly built brown shoes were fastened with laces. Unlike Miss Leigh she seemed relaxed and entirely at ease.

'There are some policemen here,' Miss Leigh told her as she approached. 'They're making inquiries about this man Parnell who's got himself murdered. They seem to think we can help.'

'Oh. Well I'm sure we'll do our best,' said Miss Brockway.

Spence watched her closely as she climbed the last few steps. Long years of habit ensured that Spence always looked at people with the eye of a man who wanted to be able to remember them later, down to the last detail. But in this case there was another reason for watching Miss Brockway closely: she was carrying a shotgun tucked under her right arm. The shotgun was a twelve-bore, Spence decided, and she carried it broken, as if she had been well taught in its use.

'This is Superintendent Spence,' said Miss Leigh. 'He's already had a word with me and I think I've told him all I can—we've just had a session in the library. Will you be wanting to ask me anything else, Superintendent?'

'Not at the moment, thank you.'

'Good. Well, in that case perhaps I can pass him and his companion on to you, Bee?'

'Certainly,' said Miss Brockway. 'Why don't you come into my study? I'll just put this shotgun away, before you get any wrong ideas, and then we can talk.'

Miss Brockway led the way along the corridor to a door opposite the library. Spence and Laurel followed her into the room.

'Don't I know you?' Miss Brockway asked Laurel with a smile.

'I used to be the Firearms Officer,' said Laurel.

'Oh, yes.' Miss Brockway nodded. 'Please sit down.'

The study was a large, comfortable, lived-in room with an open fire in the hearth. Perhaps they turn the central heating off in the holidays, thought Spence. If there is any at all.

He looked quickly around: the most noticeable feature was the profusion of photographs in frames of all shapes and sizes: some were mounted on the walls, others were standing on the desk and bookshelves. For the most part they were obviously pictures of hockey or lacrosse teams, with the occasional colour photograph of a holiday scene among them.

Miss Brockway crossed to a tall cupboard on the far side of the room and unlocked it with a key from her desk drawer. When the doors swung open Spence caught a glimpse of an ISU standard .22 target rifle, and also a revolver: Spence thought it looked like a Smith and Wesson .38.

'You have quite a collection of guns, I see,' he remarked.

'Yes, one or two. Would you like to see my firearms certificate?'

'No, thank you,' said Spence with a chuckle. 'I'm sure it's entirely in order. . . . What have you been shooting this afternoon?'

'Pigeons,' said Miss Brockway. She slotted the shotgun into position and closed the cupboard doors.

'So it's pigeon pie for supper?'

'No, I'm afraid not.' She relocked the cupboard and turned to face them again. 'They were only clay ones.' She laughed uninhibitedly, revealing white, even teeth. 'I'm not a great one for banging away at livestock, though I did plenty of it in my youth. My father was an old army man and he taught me to shoot as soon as I was old enough to hold a gun. A .22 at first, and bigger things later. But these days it's only an occasional hobby.'

Miss Brockway took off her brown suede jacket and hung it on the back of the chair behind her desk. Then she sat down, rested her elbows on the desk, and asked how she could help.

Spence explained the purpose of his visit, just as he had to Miss Leigh. 'We're talking to everyone in the locality,' he said. 'Please don't think that we're singling out you and Miss Leigh for special attention.'

'Let me get this clear,' said Miss Brockway, leaning forward suddenly. 'You and your associate are going round talking to everyone in the locality personally?'

'As many people as I can, yes.'

'But surely, most of the door-to-door inquiries are being done by your minions, Superintendent?'

'That's true, yes.'

'So in a sense Miss Leigh and I *are* being singled out for special attention.'

Spence realized that he was going to have to pay more attention to the fine print, at least where Miss Brockway was concerned. 'Let me put it in perspective for you,' he said. 'Roger Parnell lived very close to Petal Park School. And already we've found a great deal of evidence to indicate that he was unhealthily interested in your girls.'

'Oh—what sort of evidence?'

Spence took the two folders of photographs out of Laurel's hands and passed the one containing pictures of girls from the school over to Miss Brockway.

'Photographic evidence. As you'll see, it's obvious that Roger Parnell was spying on your school through high-powered telescopic lenses, probably over a period of years. Now that's something that clearly concerns you and Miss Leigh, whether you like it or not.'

Miss Brockway sounded rather surprised. 'Yes, I

can see that it would.' She opened the folder and spent some time examining the photographs in silence, switching on a desk lamp to enable her to see better. For the most part her face gave no indication of what she was thinking, except when she came to her own picture; even then there was just a muffled exclamation and a slight shaking of the head in wonder. Spence reflected how useful it must be for a headmistress to be able to hide her feelings so effectively.

'Well now,' said Miss Brockway when she had finished looking through the folder, 'I understand what you mean by an unhealthy interest. My main worry of course is for the good name of the school. Is there any evidence that these photograps have been sold or shown around the district?'

'None that I know of.'

'Good. But what I know of Parnell, which isn't much, suggests that he would not be above selling some of these shots to Soho bookshops. It's obvious enough that we didn't know they were being taken, but perhaps that adds to their attraction for a certain type of man.'

'I'm sure it does.'

'Well then, perhaps I could ask you for an assurance that if you do discover that any of these photographs have been published in any way, you will let me know about it immediately, so that I can give the girls concerned due warning. I'm sure you'll understand that some girls would consider the whole thing a great joke, but that many would be caused great distress.'

'You have my word on that,' said Spence. 'But at the moment we have no reason to suppose that anyone has seen those photos, except of course Roger Parnell himself and a few police officers. And I give you my assurance that this material will be handled discreetly while in police hands.'

Miss Brockway nodded. 'I'm delighted to hear it. . . . Will the photographs have to be shown in court?'

'That depends,' said Spence. 'But again, I'll let you know.' He passed the second folder over to her. 'There's another set of photographs here, but in this folder all the girls were aware that the pictures were being taken and they were clearly on intimate terms with Parnell. I'd like you to have a look through them and tell me if you recognize anyone.'

Miss Brockway did as she was asked and then shook her head.

'They're all strangers to you?' asked Spence.

'Mercifully, yes. One or two of the faces look vaguely familiar, as if I might have passed them in the street, but none of them was ever at the school. Not in my time, anyway.'

'All right. Now perhaps you could tell us what you and Miss Leigh were doing last night—again, I must emphasize, not because we suspect you in any way, but because we want to know whether you heard or saw anything of consequence.'

Miss Brockway thought about it. 'Well, I was invited out to dinner yesterday evening. With some people called Singleton. He's a solicitor with a daughter in the school and his wife's an old friend of mine.'

'What time did you leave and return?'

'Let's see now—I went out about seven-thirty and came back about eleven.'

'And did you notice anything unusual as you drove to and from your dinner party?'

'No. Nothing at all.'

'Did you see Miss Leigh when you came back?'

'I did, yes. We had a cup of cocoa together. We chatted for a while, and then went to bed. . . . Separately, of course.' She smiled at Spence and he grinned back.

'How did she seem?'

'Who, Vera?'

'Miss Leigh.'

'Yes, her name's Vera. . . . But I'm not quite clear what you're suggesting, Superintendent.'

'I'm not suggesting anything, I'm just asking. In order to be able to interpret correctly the information which people give me, I need to know what sort of people they are. Now—how did she seem?'

'Well—depressed. But that's not unusual.'

'Depressed because you had been invited out to dinner and she hadn't?'

'Possibly.'

'And how did Vera feel about Roger Parnell?'

Miss Brockway sighed. 'Well, I suppose you've already heard about the incident.'

'Where the windows got broken?'

'Window singular, if you don't mind. The story is now firmly established in local folklore and it gets more absurd every time I hear it. . . . However, the facts are these. We'd known for some time that occasionally, very occasionally, one or two of the girls were sneaking over to Roger Parnell's house for a necking session, or to listen to pop records or whatever took their fancy. What you must understand is that most of our pupils are day girls who live locally, and obviously some of them met Parnell quite legitimately. At parties, for instance—often quite respectable parties, given by their parents. Anyway, one day in the summer term before last, one of the boarders went over there. Nobody is quite clear what happened—we never could get it out of her—but whatever it was, she came back in a very distressed condition. And unfortunately Vera happened to find her weeping, and managed to get out of her the information that Roger Parnell was the basic cause of the trouble. So Vera stormed over there to have it all out with him, which was quite wrong, of course. There's a right way to deal with these things and a wrong way, and the way Vera did it was a mistake, which she recognizes now. Again, I'm not quite clear how it happened, but I suspect that by the time she got over there Vera was a bit hysterical. She gave Parnell a vicious shove, and in staggering backwards he pushed his elbow through a window. He cut himself, and there was some blood about, but it wasn't very serious.'

'In other words the damage both to property and person was minor?'

'Exactly. But local gossip has had Vera smashing all the windows and Parnell practically bleeding to death ever since. . . . As soon as I heard about it I went over there and tried to put things right, of course.'

'What was Parnell's reaction to it all?'

'Well, when I saw him he seemed a bit shaken, curiously enough. He seemed surprised by the violence of Vera's reaction. But he wouldn't admit that there was anything untoward about his own behaviour. His argument was that if a girl was free, white and sixteen, she could do as she pleased.'

'Did you take any action against him?'

'No. I discussed it with our solicitors, but they felt it was just something we would have to live with. And I did ask the chairman of our governors to have a word with Parnell, as one man to another.'

'That's Marcus White.'

'Yes.'

'Did it have any effect?'

'Well, I think so. Since the window incident, which was eighteen months ago, we haven't had any further trouble.' She smiled. 'At least, not until you showed me these photographs.'

Spence stood up and began to gather together the photographs on Miss Brockway's desk. 'Well,' he said, 'I think that will do for now.'

Miss Brockway helped him to return the photographs to the folders. 'But there is just one other thing,' she said thoughtfully.

'Yes?'

Miss Brockway got up from behind the desk and went and stood with her back to the fire, warming her hands behind her. 'Every school has a number of skeletons in its cupboards, Superintendent, and I suppose it's better that you should hear about this one from me rather than from anyone else. But there are two other members of my staff who had their difficulties with Mr Parnell. One of them is our caretaker, Freddie Gray, and the other is a young man who's been teaching here for just over a year, Peter Stenning.'

'Does he wear glasses and a black corduroy jacket?'

'Yes, that's right.'

Spence nodded. 'He was in the library when we came in. What's his connection with Parnell?'

'Well, Parnell was an insurance broker, as you no doubt know. And one of the lines he offered was loans secured by a second mortgage. I gather this is a very common arrangement nowadays, and highly profitable for the people arranging the loans, if not for those paying them off. Parnell used a lot of part-time agents for this second-mortgage work, and soon after he came here Peter Stenning answered an advert and began to act for Parnell in that capacity. Well, to cut a long story short, my caretaker, Freddie Gray, got himself into financial difficulties, and Peter Stenning arranged a three-hundred-pound loan for him through Parnell's company. So far so good, but after a few months Freddie forgot, as he puts it, to make one of the monthly repayments. The next thing he knew was that the finance company was threatening to sell up his house.'

'On the strength of the second mortgage.'

'Yes.'

'And so there was a row.'

'There was indeed. Freddie went to see Peter Stenning, and asked him what on earth was going on. Peter, to do him justice, was absolutely horrified. It really opened his eyes, I can tell you that. Peter went to see Roger Parnell, who told him, needless to say, that anyone who offered his house as security for a loan and then defaulted on the repayments must expect to end up homeless. Well, fortunately Peter and Freddie had enough sense to come and see me at that point. I had a word with Marcus White, who is a director of Parnell's insurance firm—'

'And he sorted it all out?'

'No he did not, I'm sorry to say. Well, not directly, anyway. He took Parnell's line, basically, which was that if a grown man freely commits himself to a contract, he can't complain when the terms of that contract are applied against him. But Marcus did suggest one possible way out. He spoke to the directors of the bank which was involved—some company I'd never even heard of—and persuaded them not to sell up Freddie's house, which apparently they were fully entitled to do. And then his idea was that the school should pay off Freddie's debt and then dock the repayments from Freddie's wages over a period of three years.'

'And was that what happened?'

'Yes. Except that on a technicality the school couldn't pay off the debt; I had to do that with a personal cheque. And so every week I get a repayment taken out of Freddie's wage packet. It suits him, and provided he stays here, which I think he will, I shall get my money back eventually. And I think Freddie appreciates what we've done for him.'

'I should hope so. What about Stenning—is he still touting for second morgages?'

'No, he isn't. I don't blame Peter for what happened, he was just naïve. He's only a couple of years out of college, and we all have to learn by our mistakes. He saw what he thought was a perfectly ethical way to supplement his income, and with a wife and a young child to support he naturally jumped at it. Once he realized that it was all a bit of a racket, he dropped out.'

'I see,' said Spence. 'Well, I'm grateful to you for telling me. And I'm sorry we've had to talk about all the problems your school has had, rather than its successes. But perhaps we can cover those some other time.'

'Yes,' said Miss Brockway with a smile, 'we do have a few things to boast about. But really, you know, if the troubles that Roger Parnell presented us with are the worst thing that ever happens to us, we shan't come to much harm.'

13

The two detectives left Petal Park School and returned to their car.

'Well,' said Laurel, 'what do you think?'

Spence buckled his safety belt. 'About what?' he asked.

'Well, Miss Brockway, for instance.'

'I think she's a smasher,' said Spence. 'I can see what interests you there all right. After this business is all over you can take back the photographs of her schoolgirls and tell her that she can destroy them—if that doesn't put you on the right road, nothing will.'

Laurel smiled as he turned the car out of the drive and on to the London Road. 'Judging by that remark, you don't regard her as a serious suspect?'

'Oh yes, I do,' said Spence firmly. 'They're all suspects, every damn one of them. The milkman, the doctor's wife, the cleaning lady, and the five hundred and one other people who also knew Parnell but who we haven't even heard of yet. I suspect them all—I rule out nobody.'

'OK,' said Laurel. 'That's reasonable. But if Miss Brockway's a suspect, what's her motive? She doesn't seem to have one.'

'Hasn't she? What about the fact that Parnell was forever leering at her girls?'

'It seems hardly adequate.'

'Well it may seem inadequate to you, Mr Laurel. But murder motives usually are inadequate, in the sense that most ordinary people would not regard them as sufficient reason for killing someone. But you have to judge motive in relation to character. That's why it's so important to get to know what kind of people we're dealing with. A motive which for one person will hardly prompt them to write a rude letter will for another person result in an overwhelming desire to kill. It's all according to context.'

Laurel nodded. 'What about Vera, then?'

'Ah, yes, the mousy Miss Leigh. Now there's an interesting character if ever I saw one. She reminds me of a girl I once danced with when I was fifteen. I made the mistake of giving her a friendly peck on the cheek on the way home and she went berserk—practically raped me in some bushes.'

'You think Vera would do the same?'

'I think she might behave rather differently with half a bottle of gin inside her.'

Laurel grinned. 'Wouldn't we all? She went a bit red in the face there, when you asked her where she was last night. Why do you think that was?'

'I don't know, unless it was because she had to tell us she had a bath. I suspect that nakedness upsets her.'

'We didn't find any saucy photos of her in Parnell's house.'

'Damn right we didn't,' said Spence. 'She's too careful by half. She's the sort of woman who carries spare elastic in her handbag. And a needle and thread.'

Laurel laughed. 'What about Vera's motive then? She obviously hated Parnell's guts. And she says she was in bed when he was killed—but she could be lying.'

'She probably was. Not about that necessarily, but about something else. You may find that a bit depressing as this case goes on—I did at first, until I got used to it. But nearly everyone we see—however innocent and however respectable they may be—nearly everyone will tell us a lie somewhere along the line. Not a big lie, perhaps—just a little white one about something they don't think is important. And the point is, you see, we always find out. We talk to a lot of people and we compare what they say about each other. And very often, before a case has gone very far, you begin to find out that not everyone is being entirely honest. And it'll depress you if you let it. Personally I refuse to.'

14

It was five-thirty p.m. when they returned to the mobile office; Spence immediately took the folders of photographs back to Sergeant Wilberforce for safe-keeping.

'Got anything for me?' he asked.

'Yes sir,' said Wilberforce. 'First of all, you ought to know that the murder weapon has been found and been sent on to Forensic.'

'You mean what you think is the murder weapon,' Spence corrected him. 'We shan't know for certain till the Lab. have done some tests.'

'There really isn't much doubt,' said Wilberforce. 'It's a heavy hammer with blood and hairs attached.'

'Where was it found?'

'Lodged in the hedge between Parnell's house and the doctor's next door. Looks as if someone threw it as far as he could in a panic.'

'Maybe,' said Spence, 'maybe. Any prints on it?'

'A full set, clear as you like. That might wrap it up pretty quickly,' he added hopefully.

'Thinking of Christmas, are you?' said Spence.

'No, sir,' said Wilberforce stoutly. 'But I expect some of the men with kids are.'

'Well, perhaps you're right,' Spence admitted. 'But

until the entire population of this country is fingerprinted, which I don't expect to see in my time, prints
are not quite as useful as you might expect, not in a
murder case. They could belong to someone who
hasn't got a criminal record, someone from the victim's
past who is entirely unknown to us. It could be months
before the investigation leads us to him—and in fact
we may never get to him. The other possibility is that
the prints don't belong to the murderer.'

'Who else could they belong to?' said Wilberforce.

'Well, the milkman, for instance. People do funny
things when they find a dead body, and they don't
always remember what they have done. If the hammer
was lying beside the body when the milkman came up
to it, he may easily have picked it up and hurled it
away in revulsion. I wouldn't be at all surprised. Anyway, Sergeant, I'm sure you've already arranged to
check the prints with records, but send someone round
to take the milkman's—if he's not on our files already.
Anything else?'

'Yes, sir. We found out where Roger Parnell spent
yesterday evening—at Big Fat Nelly's.'

'What's that, a nightclub?'

'Yes,' said Laurel. 'A smallish place but not bad of
its kind. Down on Shireport front. At this time of
year there's just a trio to play for dancing and a stripper for cabaret. In the summer it's packed out and the
prices go through the roof.'

'How did we find out he was there?' Spence asked.

'Nelly herself rang in,' said Wilberforce. 'Apparently Parnell was there till twelve-fifteen a.m., when he
left on his own. I've put some notes on what Nelly
said on your desk, but I told her you'd be in to see her
yourself tonight.'

'Correct,' said Spence. 'Now—what's this?' He peered into a cardboard box on Wilberforce's desk.

'It's the sum total of the rubbish found in the search of Parnell's garden,' said the Sergeant. 'It's going on to Forensic shortly. There's the usual refuse—some bones probably left by someone's dog, the top of a washing-up-liquid dispenser, some scraps of old newspaper. Nothing very exciting. The only remotely interesting items are a plastic comb, obviously pretty ancient, and a cuff-link.'

Spence lifted out the transparent polythene bag in which the cuff-link had been sealed. 'Looks fairly new. Just the one, was there?'

'Yes, sir.'

'It seems to be a facsimile Roman coin—or it could be a real one, I suppose.'

'No, it's a facsimile, sir,' said Wilberforce. 'But you're right, it is Roman. One of the sergeants here, Reynolds, he's a coin collector, and I got him to have a look at it. The cuff-link's gold—in colour anyway—and apparently the actual coin is silver. 46 A.D.'

Spence grunted. 'No trace of the other one in Parnell's effects, was there?'

'No, sir.'

'But then if he'd lost one in the garden he might well have thrown the other one away.'

'Or alternatively it might belong to the murderer,' said Laurel.

'In which case,' said Spence, 'all we've got to do is look for a bloke with his shirt cuff flapping in the breeze.' He dropped the polythene bag back into the carton. 'Send it all down to Forensic, Sergeant, and get the cuff-link photographed. Have the photograph shown round all the likely shops in Downsea and

Shireport and see whether they sell them, and if so who to. OK?'

'Yes, sir,' said Wilberforce. 'One other thing. . . .'

'Yes?'

'The local MP's been on the phone.'

'Marcus White?'

'Yes, sir. He rang twice, once at two o'clock and again at four-thirty. He asked to speak to you personally.'

'Amazing,' said Spence. 'And he only lives just down the road, too. What did he want?'

'I think he'd like you to go round and see him as soon as possible, if not sooner. He pointed out that after his wife had spoken to you on the phone this morning, she rang him in London and he dropped everything and returned home at once. He says that since then he's been holding himself in readiness.'

'Sounds positively obscene,' said Spence.

'He also said that he and Parnell's father were old friends, and that he and Parnell himself were business associates. And until you had discussed their business relationship with him and heard the facts, it might be as well not to mention it to the press. And that naturally he is very anxious to help all he can.'

'Which being translated,' said Spence, 'means that if there is any mud flying about he doesn't want any of it coming in his direction. However, I mustn't be cynical. . . . Did the door-to-door men call on him?'

'Oh yes, at four o'clock, sir. But he seemed to think that wasn't quite good enough. He really wants to see the top brass. And he was making occasional pointed comments about his friend the Chief Constable.'

'Let him,' said Spence. 'If he rings again you can tell him that I definitely will be seeing him, but not until nine o'clock tomorrow morning at his house. All right?'

'Yes, sir.'

'In fact you'd better ring him now and tell him anyway. . . . Is that the lot?'

'Yes, sir.'

'Thank God for that,' said Spence. 'Let's go and eat.'

15

Spence and Laurel snatched another hasty meal in the London Road police station canteen and then returned to the office.

'We're seeing Roger Parnell's office manager at eight o'clock tonight,' said Spence. 'What's his name again?'

'Dane,' said Laurel.

'Right, well until then I think we'd better start reading through some of these reports.'

The mound of typewritten material in Spence's intray was already beginning to grow. There was a report from the men who had searched Roger Parnell's house, and a whole pile of reports from the men making house-to-house inquiries, although not all of them were in yet. Spence sat down and read steadily through every page, initialling them when he had finished and passing them on to Laurel.

Unfortunately there was nothing in any of the reports which helped very much. There were just the usual bizarre bits of information which were thrown up in any murder inquiry, such as that a solicitor who lived in Petal Park Avenue owned three greyhounds which he regularly took for a walk at half past one in the morning. And that an executive who lived in a block of flats on Petal Park Road had found two people having sexual intercourse on the floor of his garage when he put his car away at ten past eleven. The last one made Spence shiver just to think about it. Apart from the copulating couple no one seemed to have heard or seen anything at all unusual.

When they had finished reading the reports Laurel pinned up a large-scale ordnance survey map of the district and marked on it the names of the occupants of all the houses visited so far, cross-referencing the map with the reports. Spence meanwhile dictated his initial report on the investigation into a pocket tape-recorder and then deposited the cassette with Percy Wilberforce. Unless the Sergeant's standards were slipping, tomorrow morning would see a copy on the desks of the Chief Constable, Dr Dunbar, the Director of the regional forensic science laboratory, and the County Coroner. There wasn't a great deal to tell them, but at least the report would reassure them that something was being done. After that, Spence dictated notes on the afternoon's interviews.

After nearly two hours of admin., Spence felt that it was time to be on the move again, and he and Laurel drove down towards the sea to meet Mr Dane at the offices of Roger Parnell's insurance-broking firm. They took with them the bunch of keys found at the scene of the murder; there was one key in the bunch which had fitted nothing obvious in Parnell's house, and Spence thought it might be the key to an office desk.

The premises occupied by Southey and Moore Ltd turned out to be in a quiet back street running parallel with one of the main shopping thoroughfares. The lights were on in both the ground-floor shop and the first-floor of the building, and when Spence rang the bell a man came quickly down some stairs at the rear of the shop and unlocked the door.

'Mr Dane?' said Spence.

'That's right,' said the man. 'I suppose you're the police officers?'

'Correct.'

'Well—come in.' Dane closed the shop door behind them and then suggested that they should go upstairs to his office.

'Lead the way,' said Spence, and they passed behind the counter and went up the narrow stairs. Once on the landing Dane turned right, through a door marked 'Mr Alec Dane—Manager' in large black letters on a white ground.

Inside the room was a slim, glamorous young woman of about twenty. She was wearing a full-length evening dress with her dark brown hair piled up on top of her head to make herself look more sophisticated. She was clearly going out somewhere special for the evening, and at the moment she was putting the final touches to her lipstlck with the aid of a small mirror.

'Oh—sorry,' she said with a smile. 'I thought I'd have finished by the time you got up here.'

Alec Dane seemed a little embarrassed by the girl's presence. 'Um—this is my sister Susan,' he said apologetically. 'She was on her way to a dance down the road when she saw my lights and dropped in for a chat.'

'Alec told me he was expecting you,' said Susan, putting away her make-up. 'But I did just want a quick word—I hope I haven't got in the way.'

'Not at all,' said Spence.

Susan pulled a short car-coat around her shoulders.

'I'll be off, then,' she said to her brother. 'I'll go and see Dad again tomorrow afternoon and tell him you'll be round in the evening—OK?'

'Yes,' said Dane, licking his lips nervously. 'That'll be fine.'

'Goodbye now,' said Susan, with smiles all round.

Spence opened the door to let her out.

'Oh—' she said, and paused.

'Yes?' said Spence.

Susan Dane glanced back at her brother. 'Oh, nothing,' she said. 'It can wait.' And with that she disappeared down the steps.

Dane invited Spence and Laurel to sit down on straight-backed chairs in front of his desk, while he himself went round and sat in a comfortable swivel chair behind it. For a moment Spence felt as if he were approaching his bank manager for a loan. He wondered if Dane were deliberately trying a bit of one-upmanship, but he rather doubted it. Alec Dane was obviously unsettled and on edge, and Spence waited in silence to see what he would say.

'Well,' said Dane at last, 'as you will appreciate, gentlemen, this has all been a very severe shock.'

'Why?' said Spence.

'Why? Well—' Dane seemed taken aback and went quite white; he had in any case a rather pale face, which was emphasized by his black hair, black frames to his glasses, and a black moustache. Spence placed him at about thirty, if that. He was tall and skinny, wearing a white shirt, what appeared to be an old-school tie, a dark-grey suit, grey socks, and black shoes, recently polished. He was not the most flamboyant dresser Spence had ever seen, and one thing Spence particularly noted was that he was not wearing cuff-links; buttons were evidently quite ostentatious enough for Mr Dane.

'Well,' Dane repeated. 'It's not every day your boss gets murdered.'

'So it was unexpected, was it?'

'Well—yes. Of course.'

'He had no enemies, no one who would be glad to see him dead?'

'No, he had no enemies. Not in the sense you mean, anyway.'

'Lovable sort of chap, was he?' said Spence. 'I mean he was running this business like a charity, letting all and sundry have things at cut rates, that sort of thing?'

Dane bit his lower lip, and for a moment Spence thought he might dissolve into tears. But after a moment he pulled himself together. 'Well,' he said, 'if you put it like that—'

'Yes,' said Spence. 'I do put it like that. And the reason why I put it like that, Mr Dane, is because I want to know the truth, not platitudes. I don't want to hear about what a fine man he was, if the truth of the matter is that he was a first-class shit. Do you get the idea?'

Dane nodded

'I'm not making any judgements about Roger Parnell one way or the other,' said Spence. 'I'm just impressing upon you that I want the plain unadorned facts. . . . Now, let's start at the beginning. First of all I'd like you to tell me when you last saw him.'

Dane licked his lips. 'Well, that would be yesterday afternoon. He arrived here about four-fifteen, left about five forty-five, when I did.'

'What were you doing yesterday evening?'

'Yesterday evening?' Dane seemed to have to think hard. 'I was at home, with my wife. . . . We watched television, went to bed fairly early because I was going to London today.'

'Why did you go to London?'

'I wanted to make a couple of business calls to discuss some new policies. But mainly, to be honest, I wanted to do some Christmas shopping. It was an excuse really. But as things turned out I didn't get any shopping done. My secretary knew what companies I was calling on, and after she rang me and told me what had happened I thought I'd better come straight back.'

'All right. Now what exactly was your business relationship with Parnell—were you partners?'

'No, I was his employee. Or to be more precise, I am employed by a private limited company of which he was the major shareholder. I'm just the office manager. Or office boy, some might say.' His mouth hardened into a straight line.

'Which company employs you, Mr Dane? I ask that question because on the plate outside the front door there are two companies listed—Southey and Moore Ltd, and Southey and Moore Life and Pensions Ltd.'

'The former company employs me, technically, but I do some work for both of them.'

'Why are there two companies?'

Dane shrugged. 'Because the directors wanted it that way. It's a common enough arrangement in the insurance business, and I suppose there are tax advantages. In practice Southey and Moore handle motor insurance, household insurance, all the orthodox stuff —that's my field, the one I know best and the one I'm most comfortable in. The Life and Pensions branch, as its name implies, takes on life assurance, unit trusts, second mortgages, and so on.'

'Who were Southey and Moore originally?'

'Well, a long time ago I suppose there were two gentlemen with those names who set up the original company. That was long before my time. I started with the company about seven years ago, when it was owned by a bloke called, Taylor, John Taylor. Taylor was an alcoholic, and he gradually drank himself to death. And as things gradually got worse I found myself doing more and more, until eventually I was virtually running the whole show.

'I see. And then when John Taylor died the firm was taken over by Roger Parnell?'

'Yes. Parnell together with Marcus White and his wife. They're the three directors.'

'Of both companies?'

'Yes.'

'OK. . . . What did Parnell read at university?'

'Oh—economics and law, I think. Some such combination. He just scraped a degree, I gather.'

'And what did he do then?'

'He worked for a finance company in the City. That gave him an introduction to money matters I suppose, and he left fairly quckly. Then he did a year as a life-assurance salesman. He was pretty good at that—very hail-fellow-well-met type of bloke. It goes down well, you know—that's the type of personality you need for that job.

'And then his mother died.'

'Yes, he got left a bit of money and the house. Came back here and bought in.'

'Did Parnell have any paper qualifications in insurance?'

'Good God, no.'

'How about yourself?'

'Oh, I'm an ACII. Sweated away at night school for it.'

'What sort of a deal have you got here—salary and a car, that sort of thing? Do you feel they treat you properly?'

'Well, it could be a lot worse.'

Laurel spoke up. 'You didn't always feel that way though, did you?' he asked.

Dane turned to look at him. 'I don't quite follow you.'

' "Dear Roger," ' said Laurel, quoting from memory, ' "This is just to say that I resign. I have had enough, more than enough, of your hypocrisy, your slimy charm, and your total lack of ethics." Remember that?'

Dane's mouth dropped open; he looked totally astonished. 'Good Lord, where on earth did you see that?'

'It's in a frame on the wall of Parnell's study,' said Laurel.

Dane shook his head in amazement and started to laugh; it made him look almost human. 'Well I'm blowed. I never dreamed that he kept that letter. I thought he would have torn it up straight away.'

'Care to tell us how you came to write it?' said Spence.

'Well. . . .' Dane pulled a face. 'I just got fed up, that's all. Moment of depression. I sent off that letter and stayed at home, started applying elsewhere. But the next day Roger came round to see me. I thought he was going to thump me, to tell you the truth, but he took it all as a great joke. He could be very affable when he tried. He said he was sorry I'd been under the weather, promised to help me out with the paper-work, take on another clerk. And offered me a rise.'

'So you withdrew the resignation?'

'Yes. Everyone was as pleased as Punch. Roger was happy, my wife was happy, and to be honest I was quite relieved myself.'

'I gather from what you said in that letter that you weren't too happy about Parnell's ethics.'

Dane shook his head. 'No, not really.'

'Explain why.'

Dane sighed. 'Well, there's a lot of money to be made in selling life assurance, pension plans, unit trusts. And if it's done in a responsible way it's a perfectly sound business proposition. But what really stuck in my throat was the second-mortgage racket. That's legal too, of course, perfectly legal, but a bit too near the knuckle for me.'

'Tell me how it works.'

'Well, briefly, let's say you're a bloke who's in debt. In theory second mortgages can be taken out by blokes who want to raise capital to start a business or something, but in practice most of the people who apply are people with bailiffs knocking at the door. So they come to us. We act as agents for what they call a fringe bank, and the fringe bank that we deal with will lend money to just about anyone who hasn't actually got a conviction for fraud—provided they're willing to offer their house as security for the loan. The interest rates are astronomical and if you default on the payments—well, they're just liable to sell your house out from under you.'

'Did you ever have a case where that happened?'

'No, we didn't, thank God, though we came close to it a couple of times. I shudder to think what the publicity would have been like if it had come to the crunch. A bloke who's in that position has only got to ring up the TV boys and they'd be round to take pictures of his kids being put out on the street in no time. Of course Roger always said that if that happened it was none of our business. We were just acting as agents in arranging the loan. The contract was between the bank and the client—and if the client was fool enough to default and the bank was ruthless enough to sell him up, then that was no worry of ours. According to Roger. An in theory he was quite right, of course.'

'But you felt differently.'

'Yes. What really worried me was, I could see myself ending up as muggins, with Roger proclaiming to all and sundry that he had no idea what I'd been up to.'

'Was he capable of that?'

'Oh yes, no doubt about it.'

'You say that this potential disaster came close to happening on a couple of occasions—'

'Yes, that's right.'

'Can you give me the details?

'No, I don't think I can. Roger just mentioned to me a couple of times that his agents had let him know that it had been a close call. He used to employ a lot of part-timers to do all the dirty work for him— going round to see people who replied to the ads, getting them to fill in the forms and so on. And what happened was, as soon as the client missed making a monthly payment, the bank would write them a really nasty letter. So naturally the client would get worried stiff and would go racing round to the agent they'd dealt with, to find out what the hell was going on. Which is one reason why you don't keep agents very long.'

'Have you got a list of the people Parnell employed in this way?'

'No, Roger used to handle all that himself. But his secretary might know where it is—I'll ask her to-morrow.'

'I believe a man called Stenning, Peter Stenning, used to work as an agent.'

'Well, I wouldn't know. I've never heard the name, I'm afraid.'

'Have you heard of Freddie Gray?'

'Freddie Gray. . . . Who's he?'

'He's the caretaker at Petal Park School. He had a second mortgage negotiated by Peter Stenning and it went sour in the way you've described.'

Dane shook his head. 'Sorry, I've never heard of him.'

'How much commission did Parnell's part-time agents get?'

'Twenty-five pounds per case. They thought they were well paid, too, but the firm got very much more than that. Two or three times as much, or more, depending on the size of the loan.'

Spence nodded. 'In general terms, was the firm as a whole doing well?'

'I should say so, yes. I'm not a director, of course, but I have a pretty good idea of what's going out and what's coming in. We moved into new offices two years ago and that was rather expensive. And the directors were taking out rather more than I would have liked. But the business is breaking even and in a few years it should be doing a lot better.'

'What happens to the firm now that Parnell's dead?'

Dane pursed his lips. 'I'm not sure. Obviously I hope it will continue. But I'm seeing Mr White and our solicitor tomorrow.'

Spence rose to his feet. 'OK. That's all for now, but we may need to see you again. By the way, did you ever visit Parnell's home?'

'Yes, a few times. Why?'

'You won't mind if we take your fingerprints then, just so that we can eliminate them from all the others in the house. Call round at the London Road police station any time tomorrow. It won't take a moment.'

'All right.'

'Oh—and one final thing. Did Parnell have a desk here?'

'Yes, he did. I've looked through it already, searched his whole office in fact. There are no personal effects there at all—just one locked drawer in the desk that I haven't got a key for.'

'Let's have a look at it.'

'All right.' Dane led the way into an office on the other side of the landing. Spence took out Parnell's bunch of keys and slotted the unidentified one into the locked drawer in the desk. It was extremely stiff to turn, and for a moment he thought it was the wrong key and that it might break. At the last moment, however, it gave way, and Spence opened the drawer.

Inside the drawer were two bundles of one-pound notes and one bundle of fivers. The bundles were as thick as they could be, given the depth of the drawer.

'Well, well, well,' said Spence. 'What's all this 'ere then?'

Dane sat down on a nearby chair with a thump; he looked haggard. 'I haven't the least idea. I had no idea it was there. No idea at all. I can't imagine where it came from or what it's for.'

Spence lifted the bundles of notes out and put them on the desk. 'Give the gentleman a receipt,' he said to Laurel. Then he pulled the drawer right out to ensure that it was empty.

It was not empty. Right at the back was a single sheet of paper, folded over twice, and a roll of 35-mm. negative film with a rubber band round it.

'Add these to the list,' said Spence. 'And do a job card—search Parnell's office. I don't suppose there's anything else here but tomorrow morning we'll have the job done by a professional. Just to make sure.'

16

Spence and Laurel pocketed their findings from Roger Parnell's office and retired to the lounge of a nearby pub. The room retained most of its original Victorian fittings, beautifully preserved, and was normally a popular spot. It was half empty at the moment, however, and Spence felt safe in examining the piece of paper from the drawer quite openly. He unfolded it carefully to reveal a handwritten list of names.

The list started with the local bishop and continued with eleven other clergymen of various denominations. Next came the editors of local newspapers, the news editors of the local television stations, and the editors of Fleet Street dailies and Sunday papers. Finally there were a number of individual citizens whose names Spence did not recognize; he could only assume that they were equally important and influential.

'What do you make of that, then?' he asked, passing the list over to Laurel.

Laurel took his time over reading it. 'On its own it could be anything,' he said eventually. 'But there was over two thousand pounds in that drawer. Taking them all in conjunction, the money, the list and the photographs on that roll of film, and it begins to look like blackmail.'

'My thoughts exactly,' said Spence. 'Let's have a look at the pictures and see what we can see.' He unrolled the 35-mm. film and held it up to the light. The film had been developed but the negatives were small and in the dim lights of the pub it was difficult to make out what they portrayed.

'What can you see?' Laurel asked after a moment.

'A man and a woman,' said Spence. 'At least I think so.'

'More nudes?'

'No, no. Fully clothed. And a child.'

'Seems innocuous enough then?'

'Possibly. But I doubt it. There's scope for a lot of scandal in a man, a woman and a child. Even with their clothes on.'

'If Parnell was blackmailig somebody, that's a very strong motive for murder,' said Laurel thoughtfully.

'Do you think so?'

'Well—yes. Isn't it?'

'Not in my book,' said Spence. 'Not unless the murderer was absolutely at the end of his tether. What's the point of killing the bloke who's blackmailing you when the police are just going to turn up the evidence? If you do that you're revealed not only as an adulterer or a homosexual or whatever, but as a murderer as well. It doesn't make sense.'

'It ties in, though,' said Laurel doggedly. 'Parnell's house was ransacked. That's what a blackmailer would do if he was looking for the evidence that Parnell was threatening him with. Perhaps he found one set of evidence, and this is a spare set. If the blackmail victim thought he'd found it all he may have felt free to kill Parnell to get his own back.'

'You haven't convinced me,' said Spence.

'All right, try this. Another possibility is that more than one person was being blackmailed. Perhaps this is evidence against one person and the killer was someone else.'

'That's a bit better,' said Spence. 'But I'm still inclined to take the gloomy view. I have a nasty feeling that this blackmail business, if it is blackmail, has nothing to do with the murder at all. It's just another facet of Parnell's lovable character.'

'What about this chap Dane that we've just seen?'

'What, as a blackmail victim?'

'No, just as an enemy. He seems to have had his disagreements wih Parnell. And if he admits to having had disagreements with him you can bet there were flaming great rows.'

'True,' said Spence. 'True. I doubt whether Dane has much of an appetite for rows, but he certainly has a capacity for bitterness, that much I'm sure of. He definitely feels he's the dogsbody in that set-up.'

'And he stands a good chance of doing well out of Parnell's death,' Laurel continued. 'He's the obvious candidate for a directorship now—in effect he'll run the whole firm, be his own boss.'

'Ah, the height of ambition,' said Spence. He took a long pull at his pint of draught Guinness. 'To be your own boss and the master of your fate. . . . Alec Dane *could* have bashed Parnell on the head, that's true. He hasn't got an alibi.'

'He's got his wife, though, hasn't he? He says he was at home with her.'

'Yes, but wives will say almost anything,' said Spence. 'For or against. Excuse the generalization, but it's largely true. You can't place any real reliance on what they say, one way or the other. . . . However, you'd better do a job card—get a man to go round and see Mrs Dane and check her husband's story. And get our bloke to ask her if she knows anyone who might have killed Parnell and why. If his previous form is anything to go by Parnell probably gave her a quick feel at some time or other, just like all the rest. She may have loved it or she may have hated it—either way she'll have some opinions about him.'

'What about the office staff?'

'Yes, good point. We want a list of names and addresses, and we'll have them all interviewed too. And the part-time agents—they probably saw the murky side of Parnell as clearly as anyone. . . . There's a lot of promising lines there. Drink up, we've got to get on.'

Laurel did as he was told. 'Where to now?'

'The station first, to drop off this roll of film and the money. We'll drag the photographer away from his fireside to make us some ten-by-eight glossies. After that we'll go on to Big Fat Nelly's.'

17

Shireport promenade was no place to linger on a windy night just before Christmas, and Spence and Laurel sat in their car for a moment to give a squall of rain time to pass. The sea rumbled angrily in the background.

Ten yards away, across the pavement, a red neon light flashed on and off above an open doorway leading to some stairs. 'Big Fat Nelly's,' it said. 'Big Fat Nelly's.'

'This den of vice we're about to go into,' said Spence. 'Tell me about it.'

'Well, they have a cabaret twice a night,' said Laurel. 'Ten o'clock and one a.m. Pretty limited at this time of year but not at all bad in the summer. If you can afford it. There's a cabaret room cum bar, rather like a small theatre, with a restaurant separate. And that's about it.'

Spence thought about it for a few moments. 'What's the position with Nelly—is she married?"

'Oh yes. Len Ford his name is. He's a big man physically but not one to make his presence felt. They're both locals, been here for donkeys' years. Her family were fairground people years ago, or so they say. Len and Nelly own this whole building now—their flat is on top, the nightclub below, and there's an amusement area at street level. All locked up at this time of year, of course.

Spence peered through the windscreen with increased respect. 'They must be worth a small fortune,' he said. 'Paying tax on about half the income it actually generates, I shouldn't wonder. Anything known?'

'Not a thing. And we've had very little trouble here either. Len usually sorts it out himself, before it gets to our stage.'

'I see. Well, let's go in.'

Inside Big Fat Nelly's it was warm and cosy, with lots of soft lights and piped music. Sergeant Wilberforce had told Nelly that Spence would be calling on her, and the staff were expecting them. They were shown into Nelly's tiny office where they perched on two bar stools against the wall, while Nellie finished a phone call.

Nelly was in her fifties, and the top half of her, which was all they could see above her desk, was enormous; Spence suspected that when she stood up she would be nearly as tall as he was, and half as heavy again. She was expensively dressed in a huge expanse of silver-grey lurex material which sparkled when she moved. Her hair was black, dyed by the look of it, and the face was cleverly made up to disguise the hard lines around the mouth. The hand that waved the cigarette-smoke out of her eyes had four diamond rings on it.

'I've got to go now,' she said into the telephone; her voice was deep and gravelly. 'I've got some gentlemen waiting.' She gave a throaty chuckle at something her caller said; halfway through the chuckle changed into a nasty smoker's cough and she put the phone down hurriedly. 'Sorry about that,' she wheezed. 'Couldn't get rid of her. . . . Now—you want to know about Roger.'

'That's right,' said Spence.

'Can I offer you a drink?'

'No offence, but no thanks.'

Nelly shrugged. 'OK. No problem. Straight down to business then. Well, Roger was here last night, and I sincerely hope he had a good time because he won't ever be here again. He was too young to die, you know —he should have had a lot of time ahead of him.'

'Did you know him well?'

'Oh, well enough. He was a good customer.'

'Maybe, but was he a good man?'

Nelly shrugged again. 'He was good in bed.'

'Yes, but that's not the same thing.'

'No, not always. . . . I'm not surprised he got hit, not really. He asked for it in some ways.'

'In what ways precisely?'

'Well, women—that's what he was interested in, and that's what causes trouble. Women have husbands, brothers, boy friends. And when a man comes sniffing around, the other fellows don't always like it. Particularly if it's a man who's known to love 'em and leave 'em. . . . I once saw a bloke get his throat cut over a woman. Years ago, in the war it was, in a pub off Piccadilly.'

Her eyes wandered away from Spence into the past and Spence pulled her back to the matter in hand. 'Did you ever hear anyone threaten him?'

'No, I can't say I did.'

'Or did you hear of anyone with a grudge against him?'

'Not that I could put a name to, no. But people used to say he was a hard businessman.'

'How often did he come here?'

'Oh, once or twice a week perhaps. Usually came about nine and had dinner.'

'On his own?'

'Quite often. But often with a girl, too.'

'The same one?'

Nelly laughed shortly. 'You must be joking. I never saw the same one twice.'

'Do you know any of their names?'

She produced a scrap of paper. 'I wrote a few of them down this afternoon when I heard the news. It's not much use, I'm afraid, but it's the best I can do.'

Spence glanced at the paper and then slipped it into his pocket. 'How did Parnell seem last night?'

Nelly stubbed out one cigarette and lit another before answering. 'A bit subdued at first. He came in about nine-thirty and drank quite a lot for him. Whisky and ginger. He had three or four, and often he only drank coke. He cheered up a bit later on.'

'He was subdued, you say.'

'Yes.'

'Depressed?'

'A little.'

'Did he say what about?'

'Yes, he did, as a matter of fact. Apparently an old girl friend of his, Jane somebody, had come to a sticky end.'

'Sticky in what way?'

Nelly shrugged. 'I gather she snuffed it. But he didn't stay gloomy very long, he wasn't the type. He soon cheered up after he'd had a good steak, and he was his normal self when he left.'

'I see. And what did he do while he was here, apart from eat?'

'Oh, chatted to people. Watched the cabaret.'

'Did he eat alone?'

'Yes, no one came with him. He got chatting to a young couple in the restaurant, though. They seemed to take him out of himself.'

'And what time did he leave?'

'Quarter past twelve. Roughly. I didn't notice at the time, but thinking about it today, when I heard, I decided it must have been about then.'

Spence turned to Laurel. 'How long would it take him to get home from here?'

'Fifteen minutes at the most,' said Laurel. 'Ten, more like.'

Spence looked at Nelly again. 'Did he leave alone?'

'Oh yes. He wouldn't find any unattached girls in here, Superintendent. I'm very particular about that.'

Spence smiled. 'No doubt. But the young couple he'd been talking to, they didn't leave with him?'

'No, they'd gone before.'

'And you didn't notice anyone go out immediately after him.'

'Oh yes,' said Nelly. 'That's why I phoned you this afternoon. I knew you'd want to know about that.'

Spence folded his arms and he leaned back against the wall. Up to that moment he had been feeling rather tired and bored; now it was all different. 'Who did you see following him out, then?'

Nelly blew a cloud of smoke at the ceiling. 'Martin Prendergast.'

'Should I know him?'

Laurel broke in. 'He's a private detective,' he said. 'I know him.'

'OK,' said Spence. 'So Martin Prendergast followed him out. What's so special about that?'

'Well,' said Nelly, 'Prendergast came in here just after Roger arrived, about half past nine. That made me suspicious for a start. Prendergast doesn't come in here very often, and when he does it's usually on business, so when I see him I sit up and take notice. The first thing he did was go straight to the phone booth in the hall. While he was in there Roger went into the gents, and when Prendergast came out and couldn't see Roger anywhere, he looked very peeved with himself. Then Roger came out of the gents again and Prendergast relaxed. Not obviously, mind you— he's no fool. But I could tell because I know what to look for.'

'I'll take your word for it,' said Spence. 'Mr Laurel, get on the phone to this bloke Prendergast and get him to come round to the station and see us.'

'What, tonight?'

'Yes, if he can make it. Use the call-box.'

Laurel nodded and left the office.

'Superintendent,' said Nelly. 'I hope you won't mind me asking—'

'Don't worry,' said Spence. 'I won't tell him who told us.'

But if Prendergast is any good, thought Spence, he's bound to guess.

18

Back in the car on the way to the station Spence shivered, turned on the heater, and wondered aloud why Big Fat Nelly had been so keen to co-operate.

'I'm not sure,' said Laurel. 'Maybe she just wants to keep on the right side of the law. Or maybe she really did have a soft spot for Parnell and wants to help catch his murderer. I think she is capable of feeling affection, despite that armour-plated exterior.'

'Armour-plated in more ways than one,' said Spence. 'Her corsets must be made of mild steel. . . . Do you think she told us the truth?'

'What about?'

'Nothing specific—just in general.'

Laurel thought about it before answering. 'Well, nightclub owners have a habit of stretching the facts to fit their fancies, but on the whole I'd say she was straight with us.'

'OK. What about this bloke Prendergast—I've never come across him before. Was he on the force?'

'No. He used to be a solicitor's clerk until he got bored with it. He worked part-time for another firm of investigators for a while and then started up on his own. He's got two other blokes working for him now, and a dolly bird in the office. He's got a good reputation and I think he's straight enough. I gather he's quite a clever businessman.'

'Well, we'll see,' said Spence. 'Did you have any trouble persuading him to come and see us?'

'No, none at all.'

'Did you tell him what it was about?'

'No.'

'OK. Well, the first thing I'm going to do when we get back is make a few phone calls. But wheel Prendergast straight in when he arrives.'

Back in the mobile office unit Spence found a note on his desk from Sergeant Wilberforce. 'Am in the dark room with the photographer—extension 281.' Spence decided to let them get on with developing the 35-mm. film in peace for the moment.

He referred to his notebook and then dialled the number of a contact of his on the staff of the evening paper published in Wellbridge, the county town. The man was just on the point of going to bed, but the prospect of getting some inside information on a murder case was sufficient incentive to secure his co-operation. He promised to let Spence borrow a number of files from the newspaper's library of cuttings; Spence then made another phone call to arrange for a police car to bring them to him.

Finally Spence dialled his home number; his wife, Julia, answered immediately. He could picture her sitting in her usual chair within easy reach of the phone, probably with a book in her lap. Their phone often rang in the evenings, sometimes for Spence, sometimes for his wife. They had no children and Julia worked as a lecturer at a College of Education; often the calls in the evening were from her students out on teaching practice, wanting advice on how to deal with a problem in the classroom. And it was partly because of Julia's knowledge of local schools that Spence was ringing her now.

'December the twenty-second is a rotten time to start a murder hunt,' said Julia. 'Any sign of a quick ending?'

'No, not at the moment.'

'And you won't be home tonight?'

'No. I'm booked in at the George in Downsea—it'll save a half-hour drive. But I shan't stay more than a night or two. If we don't get an early break I shall start coming home to sleep.'

'I should hope so too. Got your toothbrush?'

'Yes, I've got my usual bag in the boot of the car.'

'Good. I saw you on the box earlier on. Just a short interview. I suppose this man Parnell must have lived somewhere near Petal Park School?'

'Right beside it,' said Spence. 'Have you been there?'

'Oh yes, many a time. We use it for teaching practice.'

'Is it any good?'

'Well, not bad, of its kind. It's improved a lot over the last five years under Miss Brockway. Been dragged screaming into the twentieth century.'

'But it still has a very trad. approach I suppose.'

'Yes, I would say so. A lot of emphasis on manners and deportment, that sort of thing. The academic standard is quite good, as far as it goes. But they've got no science sixth form—it's a bit limited at the top end.'

'Is it expensive?'

'About average. That's the problem with these independent schools—unless they're absolutely in the top rank, with people queueing up to get in, there's a limit to what they can charge without putting people off. And if they can't charge enough then they can't raise the money to buy all the resources they need to keep abreast of new developments. It's a vicious circle.'

'But the school isn't in serious financial difficulties, is it?'

'No, I've no reason to think so. On the contrary, I should say it's a good deal more secure now than it was when Miss Brockway took over.'

'Do they pay Burnham scale?'

'Yes, but only scale one, I imagine. I don't think you'll find they have any heads of departments on scale four, as they have in the comprehensive down the road. That would be altogether too expensive.'

'So their staff are a bit weak, are they?'

'I wouldn't say that exactly. Just people for whom those sort of working conditions are more important than the money.'

'Yes, I get the picture. Now then—you women are always pretty good at estimating each other's ages—how old is Miss Brockway, would you say?'

'Bee? Getting on for forty, I suppose.'

'What did you call her—Bee?'

'Yes. I think her name's Beatrice but everyone calls her Bee—or Miss Bee if you're a pupil. She's attractive, isn't she?'

'Yes, not bad. Doesn't go out of her way to attract men, though.'

'Perhaps not.'

'Have you ever heard any whispers about her?'

'What sort of whispers?'

'Well, that she's keen on men. Or that she isn't keen on men.'

'No, not a thing. She may have a boy friend tucked away somewhere, but if she has she keeps it very discreet. And I've never heard anyone hint that she was a lesbian either, if that's what your policeman's mind is thinking.'

'No, I wasn't as a matter of fact. . . . I'm prepared to believe that some people can find a career more interesting than marriage. And affairs are often a bit of a nuisance. I accept that some people prefer to do without any entanglements. . . . So, to sum up, you'd say that Bee was an able career woman, would you?'

'Oh yes. She runs a tight ship, she's a good speaker, has a sense of humour. The parents have confidence in her. No problems.'

'What's her subject?'

'English.'

'OK. . . . Did you ever meet the chairman of the governors, Marcus White?'

'No, but then I wouldn't, would I? Chairmen of governors don't usually have much to do with the likes of I.'

'Perhaps not. What about the housemistress, Vera Leigh?'

'Ah well, Vera is rather different. She's a very old-fashioned girl.'

'What does she teach?'

'History. Spends a lot of her time doing brass rubbings and thinks like that. She told me once that she had a governess until she was thirteen—can you believe that, in this day and age? And she's only about thirty-five now.'

'But is she any good at her job?'

Julia paused. 'Well, to be fair I'd need to know more about her and the school to make a sensible judgement. But going by what I've seen of her I don't regard her as a suitable person to be in charge of the boarders. She has all the worst attributes of an old maid.'

'I see. So you don't think she's wildly successful at the non-academic side of it—but can she teach?'

'To some extent, yes. She's probably not bad with a small group of intelligent sixth-formers. But she's had no formal training as a teacher, and if she took a course now she'd probably fail.'

'Ouch,' said Spence. 'That's a hard verdict.'

'Well, it's a hard world. Believe me, Ben, if Vera Leigh were put into a co-educational comprehensive school, the kids would eat her alive in less than a week.'

Spence sighed. 'Yes,' he said, 'I suppose you're right.' He glanced through the window and saw Laurel emerge from the back door of the police station with a man beside him: presumably the stranger was Martin Prendergast, the private detective. 'Well, my love,' he said, 'the grindstone awaits my nose. Take care of yourself.'

'And you. And in case I don't see you again till it's all over—happy Christmas.'

19

Martin Prendergast was a man in his mid-forties. A report on him by one of his own inquiry agents would have read as follows: average height, slim build; brown hair parted on the left, cut short; brown eyes; small moustache; glasses with national health service frames.

He was dressed in a medium-grey suit of nondescript cut, black shoes, white shirt, blue-grey tie; he had brought with him a fawn mackintosh with a detachable winter lining. In a crowd of shoppers no one would have glanced at Martin Prendergast twice; which was, of course, exactly the effect a man in his line of work wanted to achieve. Spence admired him for it.

'I think the lateness of the hour justifies a drink,' said Spence when the introductions had been made. He opened a cupboard and took out a bottle of whisky, a soda siphon and three glasses: all these items were on Percy's list of standard equipment for the office.

While he was pouring the drinks Spence stole an occasional glance at Prendergast, wondering if he was capable of violence; he was, after all, one of the last people, if not the very last, to see Roger Parnell alive.

The conclusion Spence came to was that Prendergast was either a consummate actor, or else a man possessed of as high a degree of self-assurance as Spence had ever met. Most people who spoke to Spence in the course of his professional life were a little ill at ease: criminals because of the ever-present danger of detection and conviction, and police officers of lower rank out of respect for his own. But Prendergast was absolutely calm without being cocky; he sat very still and relaxed, and Spence wondered what sort of philosophy was behind it all: Christianity, yoga, or just a clear conscience and a good dinner? He certainly didn't give the impression of a man who was afraid he might be accused of murder.

'I expect you're wondering why we've asked you to come here?' said Spence, after they had all had a chance to take a drink.

'Presumably you think I can help you,' said Prendergast. His tone of voice was quite unrevealing of his feelings.

'Yes, we do. Detective Inspector Laurel and I are investigating the murder of one Roger Parnell. You have your ear to the ground as well as anyone in this town—we thought you might be able to fill in some gaps in our knowledge.'

'Very well, I'll try. What do you want to know?'

'I take it you knew Parnell?'

'Only by sight. I never spoke to him.'

'No, but if you knew him even by sight then you'll know that he was in Big Fat Nelly's last night.'

'Yes.'

'You know that because you were there yourself.'

'Yes.'

'I'm surprised that in the circumstances you didn't come forward voluntarily and tell us all about it.'

That didn't bother Prendergast either; he hardly blinked. 'I was satisfied in my own mind that nothing I saw or heard in Big Fat Nelly's could be of direct assistance to you. Besides, if you had been anxious to interview everyone who was there you would have said as much to the media. And no such announcement has been made.'

'It may well be made tomorrow,' said Spence. 'We may need as much information on that as we can get. . . . But let's go back to your version of last night. You're trained observer—when did you first notice Parnell?'

Prendergast looked up at the ceiling as if seeking to picture the scene. 'He came out of the gents soon after I got there.'

'Time?'

'Oh—nine-thirty.'

'And how did he seem?'

'Quiet. A bit tired perhaps. Quieter than usual, anyway.'

'You've observed him often, then?'

'No, but he has a certain reputation.'

'What did he do during the course of the evening?'

'Drank. Chatted to people.'

'Talked to you, did he?'

'No, I've already said that he didn't know me. But there seemed to be quite a few people there that he did know.'

'And what about you, what did you do all evening?'

'Had a few drinks. Relaxed. Had a meal. Watched the cabaret.'

'And what time did you leave?'

'Oh, about a quarter past twelve.'

'What about Parnell—did he leave before you or after?'

'He left before me.'

'I see. And where did Parnell go after he left?'

Not a flicker passed across Prendergast's face; Spence only hoped that his own was equally impassive. 'What makes you think I would know that, Superintendent?'

'Well,' said Spence, 'I have reason to believe that you were following Parnell. That in fact you would never have been in Big Fat Nelly's last night if he hadn't led you there.'

For the first time Prendergast's guard went down. He sighed. 'I thought I was better than that,' he said. 'And anywhere else I would have got away with it. But that Nelly doesn't miss much, does she?'

Spence waved his glass to dismiss the matter. 'Don't let it bother you,' he said. 'Parnell didn't notice and that's the main thing. . . . How long had you been tailing him?'

'Four days.'

'At whose request?'

'Ah. Well now, there, Superintendent, we have a problem. Even in normal circumstances I would be very reluctant to reveal the identity of a client without his prior permission. But in this case the client has specifically asked for absolute confidentiality. I don't even report in handwriting, let alone in the form of a typescript which my secretary would deal with.'

'I see. Well, we're very discreet too, Mr. Prendergast. I seem to be telling people that all the time, but it's true.'

'Perhaps so, but in this instance the client asked for an absolute assurance that I would not reveal his name.'

'Two points about that,' said Spence briskly. 'In the first place you had no right to give any such assurance, and judging by the answers you've given to some of my questions tonight I doubt if you did, though the client may have thought you did. Secondly, whoever engaged you to follow and report on Roger Parnell was obviously intimately involved with him in some way. And in a murder case, believe me, I am going to get to know about everyone who was intimately involved with the victim, whether they like it or not.'

Prendergast nodded. 'That's quite right and proper, of course. And I accept that having been asked for information I ought to give you all the assistance I can. But can I ask you to define more closely what you mean by being discreet? In my own case, for instance, my secretary doesn't know who I'm working for and neither for that matter does my wife. And there is nothing in writing at all. Can I ask you to observe the same precautions? In other words, not to commit my client's name to paper, and not to require a written statement from me? Unless of course it proves to be essential as prosecution evidence.'

Spence nodded in return. 'That's reasonable,' he said. 'I'll settle for that for the time being.'

Prendergast took a sip of whisky before continuing. 'All right. Well, it works like this. On Thursday last, December the sixteenth, I was approached by

Marcus White, MP, and asked to give a minute-by-minute account of the movements of Roger Parnell from that day forward, at least until Christmas.'

'And what reason did White give for having this check made?'

'Well, the story he told me was that he had been a close friend of Parnell's father, and that as both the boy's parents were dead he had given him quite a lot of help to start up on his own. He'd injected a certain amount of capital into Parnell's business, which was insurance broking, and he and his wife were co-directors of the company. But, over the four years or so that the business had been running, White had gradually become more and more concerned about Parnell's business ethics. He was now wondering whether it was politically safe to be associated with him any longer.'

'In other words, he was saying that Parnell was a crook.'

'No, it wasn't as bad as that. But he told me that Parnell was involved in the grubby end of the money-lending market, and that in his opinion this was going to backfire sooner or later. Although it was undoubtedly legal. He was also very concerned, so he said, about the increasingly lurid reports he was receiving about Parnell's private life.'

'What sort of reports?'

'Oh, there were wild rumours, apparently. Sex parties, a hint of drugs, sleeping with other men's wives.'

'OK. Go on.'

'Well, on that score alone White was wondering if it was wise to be tied up with Parnell. One thing I do know is that several of the bigwigs in White's

local party organization are very strait-laced indeed—
forever campaigning about pornography and so forth.
So I can well understand that White would not want
to be widely known as the partner of a man who
bangs as many birds as Parnell did.'

'OK. So he wanted a dawn-to-dusk report on Parnell's movements, correct?'

'That's right.'

'Reporting on a daily basis?'

'Yes. He gave me a time to telephone him each
day. Sometimes in London, sometimes at home.'

'I'd like you to give me a brief rundown of each
day you followed Parnell, just as you did for Marcus
White.'

'All right. Well we start on Saturday. I couldn't
begin on Friday, no matter how high the fee, I was
committed to a court appearance. Saturday. . . . Parnell got up late, about ten, and left the house with a
girl to go shopping.'

'She'd been there all night?'

'Unless she arrived before seven a.m., yes. After doing some shopping he dropped the girl off in Cliff
Road and then came home. Had lunch and went to
a rugger match. Came home again. Went out to dinner with another girl, brought her home, went to bed.'

'I may need detailed descriptions of these people
later,' said Spence. 'Also times, car numbers and so on,
but for the moment go on just giving me the rough
outline. Did you recognize either of these girls?'

'The Saturday morning one, no. The evening one
was a big blonde girl with long legs—I've seen her
around the town. Anyway, so much for Saturday. Sunday morning the blonde girl left about ten, looking
distinctly the worse for wear. Parnell mooched about

indoors and then went out about three o'clock and
went to the pictures.'

'Alone?'

'Yes. After the pictures he met a third girl in a
Chinese restaurant. After dinner they went on to
what I assume was her place and he left for home
about eleven-thirty.'

Spence topped up the three glasses.

'When,' said Prendergast. 'Now then—Monday. In
the morning he went to his insurance office, arriving
about nine-thirty. Stayed there all morning. Had
lunch in the Bunch of Grapes and then visited two
firms in Shireport, presumably on business. Went
home, had a meal, came back to his office and held a
briefing session for some part-time agents. I got talking to one of them later on over a pint, and I gather
they were being trained to flog second mortgages.
After that Parnell went home. Quite a heavy day
for him, I should say.'

'Now we come to Tuesday,' said Spence. 'His last
day on earth.'

'Carpe diem,' said Prendergast. 'Nine a.m. sharp,
Mrs. Tina White called on him.'

'Tina White—the MP's wife?'

'That's her.'

'And she called round at Parnell's house?'

'Yes. Stayed until eleven. There was some movement
upstairs during that time but I can't believe they were
screwing because she's old enough to be his mother,
and looks very reminiscent of a horse. But whatever
they were up to she was there a couple of hours. After
that Parnell drove down to Lime Beach and called
on a firm of solicitors. He ate an expensive lunch,
alone, in a steak house on the High Street. After that

he came back to Downsea and called in at his shower
office.'

'His what?'

'His shower office. He owns a company that installs
showers. Haven't you heard about that?'

'No. Fill me in.'

'Well, this was another thing that was worrying
Marcus White, and with good reason in my view. It's
perfectly legal but the customer gets a basically shoddy
deal. It works this way. Parnell's company puts adverts in the local press proclaiming the joys of having
a shower in your bathroom. Fair enough—he gets a
lot of inquiries. So then he has a full-time salesman
who goes around following up the inquiries, and a
certain percentage of the mugs sign up. Parnell then
sends round this jobbing plumber he sub-contracts
to, and the plumber puts in an electric water-heater
with a shower head, fixes up a curtain, and there you
are. One shower. Works pretty well, too—for a year or
so. Then it clogs up, because the water round here is
too hard, and your nice warm shower turns into a
dribble.'

'How long has this company been operating?'

'A couple of years.'

'Long enough for the complaints to have started
then?'

'Oh yes, there were lots of complaints. But they
got nowhere with Parnell, of course, so they tried the
local paper, where they saw the original advert. I have
a friend who told me that one of the brighter lads in
the news room prepared a full-scale exposé, mostly in
his own time. The arithmetic shows that Parnell must
be making a small fortune from a very small capital
outlay and about three or four hours' work a week.'

'So, if Parnell hadn't been found dead yesterday he would very shortly have been exposed in the local press for running a racket, would he?'

'No, he would not. My friend tells me that between them the advertising manager and the newspaper's lawyer decided that the story was too hot to handle— so the editor killed it.'

'I see. Parnell landed on his feet once again. . . . Did he spend the whole of Tuesday afternoon at the shower office?'

'No, he left there about three-thirty. He made two more calls on business firms and then went home. Got there about six. Had a bite to eat in front of the TV and then another girl called on him.'

Spence leaned forward. 'What time?'

'About eight o'clock.'

'How did she get there?'

'Arrived on foot.'

'Along Petal Park Avenue?'

'Yes.'

'What happened then?'

'Well, the curtains weren't drawn so I could see fairly well. I was sitting in my car all this time, by the way, watching through a pair of binoculars. They sat in the living-room and talked. No necking, they sat apart.'

'Describe this girl.'

'Aged about twenty. Slim. Shoulder-length hair, dark brown. Anorak and skirt. Not his type at all. Quite demure.'

'They were all his type,' said Spence, making a few notes on a pad in front of him. 'But at any rate she didn't go to bed with him?'

'No, certainly not.'

'What time did she leave?'

'Half past eight. A taxi called for her.'

'Number?'

'Sorry, couldn't see.'

Spence gave him an old-fashioned look.

'I mean it,' Prendergast protested. 'You have to be damn careful you know, keeping observation from a car. Especially in an area like that. People will dial 999 at the drop of a hat, and that can be very embarrassing. And how was I to know it was all going to be vital evidence in a murder case? I was just there to see what he did in general terms.'

'All right, all right,' said Spence. 'I'll forgive you, but thousands wouldn't. Do a job card, Mr Laurel—trace the taxi and that girl. I want to know who she was, and I want to know tomorrow without fail. . . . What happened next?'

'Well, after the girl had gone, Parnell went upstairs, presumably to tart himself up. And then about nine-fifteen he came out and drove down to Big Fat Nelly's.'

'And you followed him.'

'Yes. You know that already.'

Spence was silent for a few moments, thinking hard. Then: 'When you arrived at Nelly's place you phoned your client, didn't you?'

"I made a telephone call, yes.'

'And it was to your client.'

"Well, as a matter of fact it was, yes. He asked me to ring him at home any time after nine o'clock.'

'What were you supposed to do if his wife answered?'

'That's what I asked him, too. He said it wouldn't happen. The number he gave me was a direct line to his study. His wife has a line of her own.'

'Is he a wealthy man, Marcus White?'

'Oh yes. Very. Although the money comes from his wife's side, or so I understand.'

'OK. So you gave him the daily news. What then?'

'Nothing much. He just said let me know if Roger leaves there before midnight because I want to speak to him about a business matter, and if he's home in reasonable time I'll go round.'

'But Parnell didn't leave there till twelve-fifteen—so you didn't ring White again?'

'No, I didn't.'

'Did you follow Parnell home?'

'Well, if he hadn't been murdered I'd have said that I did, yes. But in fact I didn't follow him all the way. Not quite. I stayed behind him right up the London Road as far as the turning to Petal Park Road, and then he turned right and I went straight on. He was obviously going home at that point, so I felt I'd done enough for one day.'

'Hmm.' Spence sat back and considered. 'I imagine most of your work involves running credit checks on people,' he said at last.

'Most of it, yes.'

'Did you take a reading on Parnell?'

'Well, it wasn't strictly part of my brief, but yes, I did. He was known as a slow payer, but he did pay in the end. So on the whole his credit was good. I know one bank manager who had serious misgivings about him on account of his life-style, but by and large people were prepared to do business with him.'

'I see. And how did you find out he'd been murdered?'

'I was late getting up this morning—unusual for me, but there it is. When I came by Parnell's house there were police everywhere so I didn't hang around, naturally. I went straight on to my office and waited to see what developed.'

'And what did?'

'White rang me this afternoon. He told me Parnell was dead and asked for a bill.'

'No other comment?'

'None whatsoever.'

Spence grunted. 'Hmm. Anything else, Mr Laurel?'

'No, sir.'

'That's all then,' said Spence. 'We'll keep in touch.'

20

Prendergast pulled on his mackintosh with the warm winter lining and departed into the night. There was a light frost sparkling on the ground and he trod carefully as he crossed the station yard.

Spence rose to his feet and stood with his back to the electric convector-heater, warming his bottom. He glanced at his watch: it was eleven o'clock.

'It's a wonderful thing, trust, isn't it?' he said thoughtfully.

'It certainly is,' said Laurel.

'Two men in business together—you'd think they'd know each other well enough without employing private detectives. But no, apparently not. . . . Why do you think Marcus White got Prendergast to phone him every night?'

'To report on the day's doings, I suppose.'

'No. You're not suspicious enough. You're too trusting. Think the worst of everyone. Try again.'

'All right. Well—Marcus White wanted Prendergast to phone him every evening so that he could—well, so that he could find out when Parnell was out, so that he could break into his house.'

'That's better. You're beginning to think dirty, which is very necessary in a murder investigation.'

'Perhaps so, but that's not really very likely, is it?'

'What isn't?'

'Well, that a man of Marcus White's probity would break into a house.'

'Probity?' echoed Spence. 'Do you mind—we're talking about an MP, you know, not a bishop. And I wouldn't trust some of them further than I can spit.'

'All right, well let's go on thinking dirty, as you put it. What possible reason would Marcus White have for wanting to break into Roger Parnell's house?'

'I'm not sure,' said Spence. 'But I might be able to find out.' He crossed to the telephone and dialled 281. Percy Wilberforce answered from the photographic dark-room in the police station across the yard. 'Wilberforce? Any recognizable faces yet?' There was a pause. 'I see,' said Spence, and put the phone down.

'Well?' said Laurel.

'That roll of film we found in Parnell's office desk,' said Spence slowly.

'What about it?'

'On some of the pictures there's a girl with a young baby. Neither Wilberforce nor the photographer know who she is. But on nearly all the other frames there are clear pictures of a man whose face the photographer can recognize with the greatest of ease. Marcus White, his local MP.'

21

It was late, much later than Spence had intended to keep Laurel away from his teenage children, so he hurriedly sent him home with instructions to be back by eight-thirty the following morning.

The photographer had reported that the prints would take a few minutes more to dry, and while he was waiting Spence tried to clear his desk of paper. Information was beginning to pile up: it appeared, for instance, that one of Parnell's neighbours, an executive in a local boat-building firm, had three convictions for being drunk and disorderly; Roger Parnell's cleaning woman's son had various convictions for taking away cars without the owners' permission; and so on.

Spence made out a number of job cards to follow up the leads suggested by the reports and then dictated on to tape some notes on the evening's interviews with Alec Dane, Big Fat Nelly and Martin Prendergast. He had just finished that particular task when Sergeant Wilberforce delivered the set of ten-by-eight prints and a uniformed constable simultaneously delivered the files on loan from the newspaper library in Wellbridge.

Spence sent Wilberforce home too and then settled down to have a quick look through the assembled material before he went to bed himself. He opened the folder of photographs first.

There were twenty prints in all, taken on Tri X black-and-white film through a telephoto lens. The police photographer had numbered the pictures in the order they had been taken, and Spence laid them all out on his desk.

The sequence began with some shots of a young woman hanging up nappies in the garden of a sub-urban bungalow. Then there were shots of her taking the baby out for a walk in a park. Innocuous enough so far.

Next Marcus White put in an appearance; there was one shot of him getting out of a car (a Mini-Cooper), another of him going into the bungalow. This was followed by several pictures of the garden of the bungalow, with the MP holding the baby up in the air and laughing. Finally there were four frames showing the MP, the girl, and the baby, all back in the park together. In one or two cases White had his arm around the girl, but the photographs were not in themselves evidence of any immorality. They were only worth hiding away in a drawer if the relationship between the MP and the girl was one which society as a whole would disapprove of. If, in particular, Spence thought, Marcus White was the father of the girl's baby.

Time would tell. Spence returned the photographs to their folder and then turned to the files of news-paper cuttings.

The file on Marcus White was a thick one, and

Spence decided to read it just before he interviewed the MP in the morning. Instead he began by reading what the newspaper had on Roger Parnell.

Not very much, was the answer. The Shireport evening paper may have prepared an exposé on him, but the Wellbridge paper, fifteen miles to the north, had hardly heard of him. The same publisher produced a monthly glossy magazine for the county set, and Parnell's face grinned out from photographs of one or two cocktail parties and dances; but there was little else of note.

Next, Spence looked at the file on Petal Park School. The Downsea paper's accounts of various speech days were enclosed, but the file yielded nothing that Spence could relate to the murder case.

Finally, rather to Spence's surprise, there was an individual file on Beatrice Brockway, the school's headmistress. Somebody had done an interview with her shortly after her appointment. Bee had spent most of the interview tactfully pointing out the improvements she hoped to effect at the school. But whoever had written the piece had done his homework well, because he had dug up a cutting from the Wellbridge evening paper of 18 November 1952. This reported the exploits of one fifteen-year-old Beatrice Brockway, whose grandparents lived in Wellbridge. When not at school in England, young Beatrice lived on her parents' farm in Kenya, and one night during the Mau Mau emergency she had awoken to find two black men climbing in through her bedroom window.

The cutting didn't actually say so, but the impression conveyed was that the two men had been intent on rape, kidnapping and murder, not necessarily in that order. Young Beatrice hadn't panicked, however. She had just picked up the revolver which her father had taught her to use, and had shot one of the black bastards dead. In the morning bloodstains had been found outside which suggested that she had also winged the other one. Well done, Beatrice, said the *Wellbridge Evening News.*

By the time he had finished reading the file on Beatrice Brockway, Spence was tired. He felt he had done enough for one day, so he left his office and headed for the George Hotel and bed.

He wasn't doing too badly, he thought to himself. He had a victim: Roger Parnell. He had a murder weapon, even one with fingerprints on it. He also had a set of probably incriminating photographs of a leading citizen. That wasn't bad going. Finally, just to top it all off, he had at least one suspect who had been known to kill before.

The thought occurred to Spence, as he drifted off to sleep, that this case might well be settled by Christmas after all.

Thursday 23 December

22

At seven-thirty the following morning, Thursday 23
December, Spence ate breakfast in the dining-room
of the George Hotel. The Irish waitress who served
him said that it did her heart good to see him eat; she
hadn't seen a man eat like that since her brother
left home.

Soon after eight o'clock Spence was back in his office behind the London Road police station; Sergeant
Wilberforce arrived five minutes later and they con-
ferred on the programme for the day.

'At nine o'clock,' said Spence, 'I'm seeing Marcus
White, MP, at his home. After that I'm going to see
this teacher from Petal Park School, Peter Stenning.'

'The one who lives at The Lodge?' asked Wilberforce.

'Yes, that's him.'

'Do you want me to warn him to be in?'

'No, let's make it a surprise for him. If he's not at
home he'll probably be up at the school. They were
stocktaking in the library yesterday and he was help-
ing. . . . After that, let's see. . . . I'll have a word with
the school's caretaker, Mr Gray. He'll probably be
up at the school too, I shouldn't think his holiday has

started yet. And one thing you can arrange for me—I want to see Roger Parnell's cleaning lady again, Mrs Meadows. She should be at Mrs Thomson's place this morning—she cleans for the doctor's wife as well as for Parnell. Ring up Mrs Thomson and arrange for Mrs Meadows to go over to Parnell's house with me. OK?'

'Yes, sir. What time?'

'Say eleven-thirty. I should have disposed of the others by then. Oh, and let me have the keys to Parnell's house so that I can get in.'

Sergeant Wilberforce retired to his office to organize the work sheets for the day and Spence began to wade through the file on Marcus White, MP, which he had borrowed from the Wellbridge newspaper office the night before.

It emerged that White had been born in 1922. He had attended a minor public school and had served in the County Regiment during the war; he had seen enough action to make his record respectable and had risen from the ranks to emerge as a captain. Not much was said about his family background, but his father had evidently owned a small printing business, which White had gone back into after the war. He had sold the firm in 1967 for an unspecified but apparently sizeable sum.

White had first stood for Parliament in 1950, and had first been elected in 1955; he had lost his seat in '64 but won it back in '70. He had never been appointed to a Ministry and so far no honours had come his way. Someone had scrawled in the file 'a man of outstanding mediocrity', which Spence felt was not entirely fair. White evidently believed in keeping the grass-roots of his constituency happy; which was more than could be said of many politicians, and he was renowned as a fluent and powerful speaker.

The file also provided the information that Mr White had married in 1953, but had no children. His wife was apparently a keen worker on behalf of old people's homes and children's charities. White himself was a member of Rotary, a Mason, and a regular attender at the parish church; he was concerned about juvenile crime, the power of the unions, and the traffic flow in Shireport; he was against fluoridation.

The cuttings were discreet about the present state of Mr White's wealth, but reading between the lines it appeared that some eleven years ago his wife had inherited about £800,000. Apparently the bulk of Mrs White's family fortune had been made in munitions during the first world war; that made it slightly grubby money, but a lot of money nonetheless. Spence estimated that taking into account the proceeds of the printing business, and given reasonably competent financial advice over the last ten years, the Whites ought to be worth well over a million by now. In which case, he thought, what are they doing living in Petal Park Avenue? From what Spence had seen of it so far the district seemed exclusive, but not millionaire territory.

Having gutted the file for the information he needed, Spence handed it over to Percy to be returned promptly to its owner, together with the files he had read the night before.

At twenty to nine Laurel arrived and Spence immediately showed him the photographs which had been printed from the 35-mm. film found in Roger Parnell's desk. Laurel studied them thoughtfully.

'So,' he said when he had looked at them all, 'you think that these photos, plus the list, plus the money, all add up to blackmail?'

'At the moment I do, yes,' said Spence.

'Well if that's so, why weren't there any prints from the film in the drawer with the film itself?'

'Oh, I can think of lots of reasons. Perhaps Parnell developed one set of prints to see what he had, and then sent them to White with the first demand for money. After that he didn't need any more prints until and unless White refused to pay.'

Laurel shook his head. 'I'm still not convinced,' he said. 'Somehow it just doesn't feel right. I accept that Parnell was obviously spying on White—he must have been to end up with photographs like those in his possession. But I can't see Parnell as a blackmailer and White as a victim. Everything I know about White suggests that he wouldn't knuckle under like that.'

'He may not have had much choice,' said Spence. 'But I won't prejudge the issue. It may be that Mr White can convince me that he wasn't being blackmailed—but he's going to have to do some pretty fancy talking. . . . Have you had any dealings with him before?'

'Not directly, no. But he always lets us know when he's going to be away so that we can keep an eye on his house. And I make damn sure it is well looked after too, because he's got a lot of very valuable property. And if anything went wrong in those circumstances he'd be a very difficult man to deal with. People who cross him do not prosper.'

'So you have some sympathy with Martin Prendergast, then,' asked Spence. 'He's obviously very anxious that White shouldn't know he's told us that White is employing him.'

'I'm not surprised,' said Laurel. 'If White knew that Prendergast had given him away he'd do his utmost to ruin him, I'm sure of that. And White is a man who carries enough clout in this town to do a great deal of damage.'

'OK. Well, when we see White together let's handle it this way. I'll do all the talking and I'll take all the bricks he throws back. And since this is your patch and you're probably going to have dealings with him in the future, you can throw me disapproving looks from time to time. We'll take the photos and a Xerox of the list of names and see how he likes them for openers.' He glanced at his watch. 'And if we want to be there on time we'd better be on our way.'

23

On a map, Petal Park Avenue formed the upper three sides of a square, with Petal Park Road as the fourth side, at the bottom; the Avenue first ran north from Petal Park Road, then due east, and finally south again to rejoin Petal Park Road. Roger Parnell's house was positioned on the north-west corner of the square, and Marcus White's on the north-east.

Spence and Laurel drove to the appointment in Laurel's car, and they had no sooner turned into the drive which led to the MP's house than Spence realized that he had been quite wrong in thinking that Petal Park Avenue was no place for a millionaire to live. At the entrance to the estate, tall wrought-iron gates formed a break in a six-foot-high stone wall which had recently been repointed. The house itself lay at the end of a one-hundred-yard tarmac drive which wound its way through a copse of trees; and when it did appear, the house was the sort of mansion which was advertised in *Country Life* as providing ten bedrooms and five bathrooms.

When he and Laurel got out of the car Spence could see at once that no expense had been spared either on the building or on the garden. The lawns were beautifully landscaped and stretched away to woodland, which in turn hid nothing more disconcerting than the local golf course. The paintwork on the house was new and all the windows were double-glazed; the garage was large enough for two other Rolls Royces in addition to the one which stood outside. To the left of the house was a large greenhouse, and beyond it was the bright glint of the tiles of an open-air swimming pool, now drained for the winter; beside the pool was a log hut which Spence took to be a sauna bath.

Spence's guess was that if the interior of the house matched up to the exterior, and if Marcus White was paying his taxes, he would be needing every penny of income from his million pounds just to maintain his life-style.

Spence rang the doorbell and waited. After a few moments the door was opened by an elderly woman in black who was unmistakably the housekeeper. She undertook to let Mr White know that they had arrived and asked them to wait in the hall.

The hall itself covered an area equal to the ground floor of many normal houses, and several large radiators produced an almost tropical heat. Spence took off his overcoat and examined the pictures on the walls. One of them was an oil painting by a local artist named Smith, whose works were sufficiently respected to sell for three hundred pounds each; Spence knew that because his wife had bought him one as a present two years earlier.

After about five minutes a door opened and Marcus White himself appeared. He was of slightly less than average height, with a thickening waistline which his tailor had worked wonders to disguise. His complexion was deeply tanned, and Spence suspected the

frequent use of a sun lamp. White's hairline was re-
ceding, and such hair as was left was carefully parted
and combed to hide the baldness on top; he had a
small brown moustache. The colour scheme established by the bronzed appearance of White's face was
carefully continued in a dark brown three-piece suit,
brown suede shoes, a white shirt with gold cuff-links,
and a silk tie striped in gold and silver.

'Detective Superintendent Spence?' asked White,
looking from one man to the other.

'That's me,' said Spence.

White gave him a look which would have made
most lesser men quail. 'Before we start,' he said om-
inously, 'I'd like a word with you in private. In my
study.' He crossed the hall, opened a door and went
inside.

'Just like being back at school,' said Spence to Laurel as he went by. 'Wait out here for the time being.'
He entered the study and closed the door behind him.

'Well now, Spence,' said White briskly, 'I thought
I'd say this to you on your own, before we start, because I don't like to show men up in front of their
subordinates.'

'That's very kind of you,' said Spence. 'I really appreciate that.'

If Marcus White detected any hint of irony in
Spence's tone of voice he decided to disregard it. 'I
want to make something clear,' he continued. 'I was
a business associate of Roger Parnell's, and also a
personal friend of his. I knew his father from way
back. . . . Early yesterday morning I went to London,
but immediately my wife phoned me and told me
what had happened I cancelled all my appointments
and came straight home. I sent two messages to you

yesterday afternoon, confirming my availability, and as one of the people who knew Roger Parnell best I was an obvious source of reliable information. Yet you didn't even bother to come and see me.'

'Two of my men called on you yesterday,' said Spence. 'And I'm here now.'

'Two constables' said White as if to be a constable was to belong to a caste of untouchables. 'Which was not only discourteous, it was also grossly inefficient. I'm sorry but I'm afraid I shall have to make my feelings on this matter clear to the Chief Constable.'

Spence sighed. 'Very well,' he said. 'If you insist on plain speaking let me make something equally clear. For some years now the Chief Constable has delegated a large measure of responsibility for most murder investigations in this county to me. He has instructed me in writing to conduct such investigations without fear or favour, and that is what I intend to do.'

'Are you suggesting that I am asking favours?' snapped White. 'Because if so that is very far from being the case.'

'You have just threatened to report me to the Chief Constable,' said Spence patiently 'and in my experience threats emanate from those with something to hide. The effect of such a threat is not to intimidate me, it is to make me suspicious.'

White's cheeks began to turn a dangerous red, and Spence wondered what his blood-pressure was like.

'In your case,' Spence continued 'I already have evidence in my possession which strongly suggests that you were being blackmailed by Roger Parnell. And blackmail is a possible motive for murder.'

For a moment Spence was afraid that White would

have a stroke. He rocked on his heels and his whole
face became suffused with blood.

'Blackmail?' he spluttered. 'Poppycock!' He blurted
out the word so fiercely that globules of spit were dis-
persed in all directions. 'I've never heard anything so
outrageous in all my life! What in God's name are you
talking about?'

Without a word Spence opened the folder he had
brought with him and held up a photograph of Marcus White with the girl and the baby in a park. White
approached a step or two closer to be sure of what he
was looking at; he stared at it for some moments and
then turned his eyes to Spence.

'Where did you get that?'

'Who is the girl in this photograph?' said Spence.
'Tell me about her.'

White's eyes became glassy, like the eyes of a boxer
who has taken one punch too many. He turned away
and almost staggered to the window; his shoulders
were bowed. There was a long pause.

'You're quite wrong,' he said at last. 'Quite wrong.
There was no question of blackmail. Absolutely no
question whatever.'

Spence moved closer to him. 'I'd like you to fetch
your wife in,' he said. 'I'd like to hear what she has to
say too.'

"My wife?' White glanced at Spence over his shoulder, and then looked back out of the window. 'Oh
no, I don't think so. There's no need to involve her.'

'On the contrary,' said Spence, 'her presence is
essential. I want Detective Inspector Laurel in here
too.'

White came away from the window with the greatest

reluctance. 'Oh, very well,' he said. 'If you insist.'

He left the study, moving very slowly, and after a moment Laurel came in; he looked distinctly apprehensive himself. 'Trouble?' he asked quietly.

'Nothing we can't handle,' said Spence. He sat down and Laurel uneasily joined him.

Nothing further was said for some minutes. Spence passed the time by making a rough valuation of the antique furniture in the room: it worked out at £14,000.

Eventually White returned with his wife and introduced her to the two police officers. His attitude was calmer now, neither as pompous and arrogant as he had been at first nor as shocked as the photograph had left him.

'I believe you've spoken to my wife on the telephone,' said White as he sat down.

'Just the odd word,' said Spence.

Mrs White smiled politely, and to his surprise Spence thought he detected a glint of amusement in her eye. It clearly wasn't every day that her husband had the stuffing knocked out of him, but the experience didn't seem to have upset Mrs White at all.

Tina White was at least fifty, Spence decided, a pear-shaped woman with a small bust and large hips; her legs had a tendency to thickness at the ankles. She had brown hair, cut close to her head, with a touch of red in it. The eyes were blue and rather prominent, and her face might best be described as unfortunate: it was asymmetrical, as if one side of her jaw had been damaged when she was a child; when she spoke the teeth were revealed as uneven, with occasional flashes of gold.

The plain fact was that Mrs White was an ugly

woman, but Spence was in no doubt that there was a lot of force in her personality; and although her figure was far from perfect she carried herself with style. Where clothes were concerned she undoubtedly had enough money to pay for the best of everything, and this morning she was wearing a dark green dress with short sleeves and a belt at the waist. Spence couldn't identify the material, but its quality and cut were of the highest. She wore strong shoes laced up high around the ankles, and to complete the ensemble there was a diamond brooch above her heart and a platinum watch on her left wrist. She sat very erect, with an awareness of deportment which had no doubt been dinned into her as a child.

'Well,' said White, sitting with his hands on his knees, 'let's hear what you have to say.'

'A few general questions to begin with,' said Spence, addressing himself to the MP. 'First of all I'd like to ask you where you were on Tuesday evening.'

'At home,' said White.

'Both of you?'

'Yes, from about two p.m.'

'Did you have any contact with Roger Parnell on Tuesday afternoon or evening?'

'No—why should I?' asked White.

'You were a business associate of his.'

'Well, yes, that's true. But anyway we saw nothing of him. Neither of us.'

'How did you come to know Roger Parnell in the first place?'

'Well,' said White, 'his father worked for the party for years. A first-class man. After he died I always kept a friendly eye on the family, and they certainly had their share of troubles. Roger's brother was killed in

Northern Ireland, then his mother died, and after that he came back here and wanted to set up his own business. He had a little capital but not enough to make real headway, so my wife and I chipped in. It's always been my policy to support up-and-coming young men, that's what this country needs.'

Mrs White broke in. 'I don't think the Superintendent wants to hear about politics, darling.' She glanced at Spence, again with a hint of amusement, and lit a cigarette with a gold table lighter. White said nothing but looked glum.

'It was as simple as that then, was it?' said Spence. 'You just helped him because of your friendship with his father?'

White looked at Spence intently. 'What are you getting at, Superintendent?'

'What I'm getting at is the fact that Roger Parnell was young and inexperienced. When you put money behind him you were investing in a very risky venture.'

'Wrong,' said White firmly. 'And in any case it couldn't have mattered less if we'd lost every penny. We made a decision to give a young man his chance, that's all. We didn't approach it on a profit-and-loss basis, though as it happens we have shown a profit. The firm is doing quite well—or was until yesterday.'

'There was no question of duress, then?'

'Duress?'

'You didn't feel under any pressure to support him financially?'

'No. Certainly not. . . .' White paused and then seemed to feel that some further explanation was necessary. 'Look here, Superintendent, you don't seem to realize how concerned I am about this business. Very concerned indeed. My only interest in this matter is to see justice done, to help catch Roger's murderer. That's all. Now, my wife and I had a little chat before we came in here, and we decided that I ought to put my cards on the table.'

'That's not a bad idea,' said Spence.

'Perhaps you'd like to show my wife the photograph you showed me a few minutes ago.'

Spence did so.

'Can you tell us where you found it?' White asked.

'It was found in a locked drawer in Roger Parnell's desk at his office. Or to be more precise, a roll of film was found there, and this is a print from it. We also found a list of prominent people and a large sum of money.'

'All of which, to your mind, suggests blackmail?' said White.

'It does.'

White fingered his moustache nervously. 'I give you my word, Spence, there's no question of that. No question at all.'

'Unfortunately,' said Spence, 'your word alone is not good enough. I want to know who the girl is.'

Marcus White stood up abruptly. 'You tell him about it,' he said to his wife. 'I'll be back in a minute.' And he walked hurriedly out of the room.

24

The MP's wife put the photograph down in her lap and folded her hands over it. 'Superintendent,' she said. 'You have contrived to disconcert my husband. And that is not an easy thing to do, believe me.'

'Who is the girl?' said Spence. 'The mother of that baby. That's what I want to know. It's a simple question.'

'Indeed it is, but not so simple to answer. . . .' She crossed her legs. 'You see, if I say that the girl is Marcus's mistress then it sounds so sordid, doesn't it? Let's just say that she's a girl he met some years ago and fell in love with. As is the way in these things, he set her up in a flat, gave her some money, and they were both very happy. And in case you're wondering, perhaps I'd better say that he told me all about her, even at that stage. We have no secrets from each other, Superintendent—we're too old and too wicked for that.'

'And then, I suppose, after a while, the girl just got pregnant?'

'Yes.'

'I see. . . . Deliberately?'

Mrs White reflected. 'I'm not sure. She may have

had a mixture of motives. But in any case, she decided she didn't want an abortion and neither did Marcus. I couldn't have any children, you see, and I wouldn't have wanted them if I'd been able to. But Marcus always did. So we talked it over, and we decided that she'd better go ahead and have the child. He bought her a bungalow about thirty miles away and he sees her every few days. The baby calls him Grandpa, and everybody is very happy. A man of his age and position could do a great deal worse, you know.'

'Bit dangerous though, isn't it?' said Spence. 'An MP with a mistress and an illegitimate child? The papers would make a real meal of that.'

'Oh, of course they would,' said Mrs White. 'Of course. And naturally, Superintendent, we'd prefer not to have it printed on the front page of the *News of the World* if we can possibly avoid it. It would ruin Marcus's career, such as it is, and he'd never get a knighthood, which is his secret ambition. But then I always feel that everyone, without exception, everyone has got something in their life which they would prefer not to be public knowledge. Don't you agree? And for a middle-aged man to fall deeply in love is hardly a crime.'

'Nevertheless,' said Spence, 'if this folder of photographs were circulated to all the prominent people who are listed on the sheet of paper which I found in Parnell's drawer, then the embarrassment to yourself and your husband would be considerable.'

'Indeed it would.'

'And there was a large sum of money with them. How do you explain that?'

'Roger preferred cash to cheques every time. He

liked the feel of it. I'm not surprised that he had a little store of it somewhere.'

'Just that?'

'Yes.'

'I think I should warn you that I'm having the numbers of these notes traced.'

Mrs White smiled and nodded her head. 'Yes,' she said, 'I can see your line of reasoning. And I don't blame you for thinking the way you do. But I assure you categorically that the notes will not be traced back to us. I am absolutely confident of that for two reasons. First, because if Roger had wanted any more money from my husband and myself he wouldn't have needed to blackmail us—he could have just asked, and we would have given it to him. And secondly, I know there were no blackmail payments being made, not of any size anyway, because, not to put too fine a point on it, I control the money in this family. If anyone was putting the squeeze on my husband I would be certain to know.'

Spence changed tack. 'All right, let's put it another way. Was Roger Parnell capable of blackmail?'

'Oh yes. He was. He was not only capable of blackmail in general, he was even capable of blackmailing his closest friends, such as ourselves. I have no doubt that he contemplated it. After all, he did secretly follow my husband and take those photographs that you've got there. Marcus didn't pose for them, you know. And apparently, from what you say, Roger did spend a few idle moments listing the sort of people he might threaten to send them to. But I'm not really surprised by any of that. Roger Parnell was a bastard, Superintendent—but he was a very lovable bastard. I was very fond of him myself—I won't say I loved him —but I'd pay a lot of money to see his murderer caught. And in my opinion it's a pity they've done away with hanging.'

25

Marcus White returned a few moments later. Spence caught a whiff of whisky as the MP passed his chair, and judging by the puffiness around his eyes he had been weeping.

'I'm sorry to have had to go out like that,' he said quietly. 'But it's a bit of a shock to find that you've been spied upon by someone you regarded as a friend.'

He means it too, thought Spence. The idea that Roger Parnell would have felt exactly the same way if he had ever found out about Marcus White putting a private detective on his tail obviously never crossed the MP's mind. He wasn't being hypocritical—it was just that it never occurred to him that he himself was guilty of a sin which he found deeply offensive when committed by someone else. Spence marvelled at the mind of a politician.

'Tell me more about this friend of yours,' said Spence. 'What was Parnell's relationship with Petal Park School, for instance?'

White looked blank. 'He had no connection with the school at all.'

'On the contrary, he was intimately involved with it. I know for a fact that Miss Brockway had to ask you to speak to him about his relationships with her girls.'

'Oh, that, yes.' Spence was quite certain that the man had genuinely forgotten. 'Yes, you're quite right, there was that. But the truth of the matter is, it was a lot of fuss about nothing. These schoolmarms, you know, they do get things a bit out of perspective. I just asked him to be a bit more discreet, that's all.'

'I see. What about Parnell's standing in the business community—respected, was he? Or did they think he was a bit too sharp for comfort?'

'I wasn't aware of any problems in that direction. He was a member of the relevant professional body— they do have standards of conduct, you know.'

'I imagine they do, but you're wrong in thinking that Parnell had any formal qualifications in insurance. He didn't. On the other hand, his office manager does have some letters after his name.'

White sighed irritably. 'Oh, well, perhaps you're right. But Roger was very able in his chosen field, that much is quite certain.'

'Did you know that the firm was negotiating second mortgages?'

'Among other things, yes.'

'Some of the adverts I've seen look distinctly misleading to me.'

White sat up straight and spoke more briskly. 'That's a matter for the newspaper concerned. There again, there are guidelines on these matters—it's up to the editor to see that nothing appears in his paper which goes outside them. And in any case, I don't acknowledge that the firm's adverts were misleading, in any way, shape or form.'

He's beginning to get his nerve back, thought

Spence. 'Did you know that Parnell ran a company installing showers?'

'I did, yes.'

'Were you happy about the way that firm conducted its business?'

'I know nothing whatever about it. Roger mentioned to me some time ago that he was thinking of setting up such a company, and asked me if I would like to be a director. I declined.'

'Why?'

'Because the last time I counted I was a director of seventeen companies, and that's more than enough.'

'There have been numerous complaints about Parnell's shower company. And a lot of people who arranged second mortgages through Southey and Moore are wishing they hadn't.'

Marcus White shrugged. 'I can't speak about the showers, but the insurance-broking business handles an enormous number of accounts. There are bound to be a few complaints. If anyone had complained to me direct I would have investigated, and if the complaint was justified I would have put it right.'

'But someone did complain. Miss Brockway complained to you that the caretaker at her school, Mr Gray, was getting the dirty end of the stick on a second-mortgage deal.'

White didn't even pause for breath. 'Exactly. There's a case in point. If I recall correctly, I suggested to her a way in which the matter could be resolved to everyone's satisfaction.'

Spence realized that on this visit at least he was going to get no further change out of Marcus White. It was time to move on. The contest could always be renewed later, possibly in the London Road police station, where White would very probably feel less confident than he did here.

'To summarize, then,' said Spence, 'on Tuesday evening you and your wife were here in this house together, the whole time?'

'That's correct.'

'There was no one else here?' White shook his head. 'I presume you have both visited Parnell's house in the past?'

'Frequently. Why?'

'I take it you'll have no objection to letting us have your fingerprints in order to eliminate them from all the others?'

White's fingers tapped on his knee but he accepted the point. 'No, we would have no objection to that.'

'Very well, then, I'll send someone round later today. Oh—and one last thing. Do you own a pair of cuff-links made out of two old coins? Either genuine or facsimile.'

'No, I'm quite certain I don't. Why do you ask?'

'Did Parnell own such a pair of cuff-links?'

'I've no idea. How on earth would I know that?'

'Mrs White?'

The MP's wife frowned thoughtfully. 'I can't say that I ever saw Roger wearing cuff-links such as you've described, Superintendent. But I've seen the kind of thing you mean, in shops.'

Spence rose to his feet to leave and White stood up with him. He was almost his normal bombastic self again.

'You know, Superintendent,' he said, 'I can't really think why you've bothered to question my wife and

myself at all. It's pretty obvious what happened—
thieves broke into the house and Roger interrupted
them. They panicked and killed him.'

'How did you know anyone broke in?' asked Spence.
'We haven't released that information.'

'Oh, really, Superintendent.' White was openly
contemptuous. 'Don't be any more ridiculous than
you need. The whole neighbourhood knows all about
the broken window and the state of the house. I think
my housekeeper knows more about this case than you
do. And it wasn't me or my wife who broke in and
clubbed Roger to death, I assure you—it was some
small-time thief. If you take my advice you'll pull in
all the local hooligans and yobboes and question them
till the pips squeak.'

'I'm glad you feel like that,' said Spence. 'Because
that's exactly what I am doing.'

26

Back in the car Spence used the radio to arrange for Sergeant Wilberforce to send a man round immediately to take Mr and Mrs White's fingerprints. Then he asked Laurel to drive out into Petal Park Avenue and park the car at the side of the road. Laurel did so, bringing the car to a halt in a welcome patch of sunlight. The avenue was deserted and the world seemed very peaceful.

'I want to think this thing through before we go any further,' said Spence. 'I find it doesn't pay to go charging along at full speed the whole time—you're inclined not to see the wood for the trees. . . . Now then, let's see where we've got to. . . . We have a victim, Roger Parnell. Popular with most people, especially the ladies, but a man who made a few enemies. He was inclined not to be too fussy about how he made his money, and he certainly wasn't too particular who he offended when it came to girl friends. In that field he just went his own way and to hell with the consequences.'

'And as Big Fat Nelly reminded us,' said Laurel, 'girls tend to have brothers and fathers and boy friends who may not like that approach.'

'Precisely. Let's file that thought away for the

moment and look at the suspects we know about.
First of all there are Mr and Mrs Marcus White,
whom we've just seen.'

'Well, he's a promising customer for a start. He's
our best bet if you ask me.'

'Maybe,' said Spence. 'But his wife says he was at
home all evening. How are you going to argue away
that?'

'I thought you said that what wives said should be
ignored?' protested Laurel.

'I ignore it, yes,' said Spence. 'But juries don't. If
Mrs White got up in court and crossed her heart and
swore that her husband was beside her all night, can
you see a jury saying otherwise? I can't. Anyway,
what's his motive?'

'Blackmail, of course. I know they deny there was
any blackmail, but then they're hardly likely to admit it, and the evidence is very persuasive.'

'You didn't think so an hour ago.'

'No, well, perhaps not. That was before I heard
what he had to say, and a lot of it was bluster. White
is a man who obviously married for money, and he
clearly spends huge quantities of it, so naturally he
wouldn't take very kindly to being blackmailed.'

'I accept that,' said Spence. 'I don't like blackmail
very much as a motive, as you know, but Marcus
and his wife could be in it together, there's no doubt
about that. It'll be interesting to see how their prints
compare with those on the hammer.'

'They didn't object to having them taken.'

'No, but then no one outside the force knows that
the murder weapon has been found yet. So Marcus
White and his wife are possibles for the time being.
Who else?'

'Well, there's the woman who did Parnell's cleaning for him,' said Laurel. 'Mrs Meadows. Her son's got a record. She could have told him all about the goodies in Parnell's place, the cameras and so on, and he may have fancied his chances. Or perhaps some of his pals.'

'You're back to the old thieves breaking in and being interrupted theory again,' said Spence.

'Well, why not? It's a possibility.'

'So it is,' said Spence. 'So it is. And I did a job card last night to have young Meadows interviewed today. And I've arranged for Mrs Meadows to be available a bit later on to go over Parnell's house with us. I want to see if anything really has been stolen, and we can ask her who she discussed Parnell with then. . . . And then there's that lot over there.' He nodded towards Petal Park School. 'We mustn't forget them. There are at least two very good suspects in the park, possibly more.'

'Vera Leigh. . . .'

'And Bee Brockway. Both of them quite capable of swinging a hammer with sufficient force to do the damage, and neither of them having an alibi.'

'They haven't really got a strong motive, though.'

'Oh yes they have,' said Spence. 'Parnell was banging their girls—that's more than enough. They both play it pretty cool with us, but I'm willing to bet that in private they both got very het up about that filthy beast Parnell.'

'Yes, I expect you're right,' said Laurel. 'And that study of Miss Brockway's was just crowded with photos of all her girls—hockey teams and holiday snaps and heaven knows what else. I should imagine she feels pretty protective towards them.'

'And for that matter,' said Spence, 'there may be other members of their staff who felt even more strongly about Parnell than they did. We haven't interviewed them all yet, by any means. Although that fellow Peter Stenning is next on my list.'

'He's the one who was a part-time agent for Parnell, isn't he?'

'Yes. And we must think about his wife too, of course. Remember how she came belting up here in that minivan of hers, first thing yesterday morning?'

'Oh yes. She seemed a bit keen on Parnell.'

'Damn right she did. And her husband may not have appreciated it either.'

'What about Parnell's nearest and dearest?' said Laurel.

'Mostly dead,' said Spence. 'But I agree, that's normally where I start looking for a murderer, among the victim's immediate family.'

'If I remember rightly, he's got a married sister in the USA—'

'And an uncle in Birmingham. And that's about it. But get Wilberforce to check that both those two really were miles away when it all happened. If we suddenly discovered that they were both staying with friends here in Downsea on the night in question we should look rather stupid. I know Wilberforce spoke to the uncle on the phone yesterday morning, but get him to have an independent check made as well.'

'OK. . . . How about Alec Dane?'

'Yes, I suppose he was Parnell's closest business associate. And I think he'd had his fill of Parnell over the years. I've got somebody seeing his wife this morning—she may shed some light on the matter.'

'We ought to have Martin Prendergast looked at

too—see if he had any earlier dealings with Parnell. He claims that he never spoke to him, but for all we know they may have been bitter enemies over something or other. And Prendergast could easily have followed him all the way home and not gone straight up London Road as he said.'

Spence sighed. 'True,' he said. 'Very true. And then there's that girl Prendergast told us about. The one who visited Parnell just before he went out to Big Fat Nelly's. Arrived at eight o'clock and left at eight-thirty by taxi. I'd really like to find her and hear what they talked about.'

'Is somebody working on it?'

'Oh yes, don't worry. . . . Well, let's drive round to the school and see Peter Stenning and the caretaker, Freddie Gray. You never know your luck—one of them may fall down on his knees and confess.'

27

It was ten thirty-five when Spence and Laurel arrived at the Stennings' house: it stood at the head of the drive leading to Petal Park School, and faded white paint on a sign above the front door proclaimed its name as The Lodge. Spence pressed the bell-push and was surprised by an old-fashioned clanging within.

The door was opened by Dawn Stenning. Her blue eyes blinked at them for a moment from behind her glasses, and she brushed her blonde hair to one side as if to see them more clearly. 'Oh,' she said. 'More policemen. You're the ones I saw yesterday morning, aren't you?'

Spence nodded and looked at her closely. She was wearing a white roll-neck sweater, brown slacks, white socks and brown shoes. Spence could see more of her figure now than he had been able to the previous day, and he could see that she was the kind of girl who habitually stood or sat so that her bust stuck out. As busts went, hers was quite an attractive one; the face, on the other hand, could not have been called beautiful, but her expression was alert and lively.

'May we come in?' asked Spence.

Dawn hesitated briefly and then shrugged. 'Oh, I suppose so,' she said. 'Though I can't think why. We said all we had to say to the other two yesterday afternoon.' She stood to one side to allow Spence and Laurel to enter.

'Is your husband in?' Spence asked.

'Yes, he's in the living-room. Follow your nose, it's straight ahead.'

Spence walked through the entrance hall; it was dark and depressing: the house had not been decorated for a long time, and whoever did it on the last occasion had evidently bought a large quantity of chocolate-brown paint in a sale. He pushed open the door immediately ahead of him and went into the living-room.

Inside the room Peter Stenning was rising awkwardly to his feet, a copy of the *Daily Express* clutched in his left hand. A small coal fire was burning in the hearth and a clothes-horse covered with wet clothes stood in front of it; the atmosphere felt damp.

'You'll have to excuse the mess,' said Dawn, following them in. 'If we'd known you were coming we'd have tidied up a bit.'

Spence nodded a greeting to Peter Stenning, who nodded nervously back. Like his wife, Peter had thick lenses in his glasses to correct his myopia. He looked very young, about twenty, though Spence knew that in fact he must be a few years older than that. He was slim, slightly less than average in height, and he had brown, straight hair of medium length. He was wearing a green shirt and a brown and green terylene tie with a square end; Spence thought it looked as if someone had given it to him for Christmas ten years earlier. Brown trousers and a pair of beaten-up slippers completed his outfit, and the black corduroy jacket which he had been wearing at the school the previous afternoon hung over the back of a nearby chair.

'Sit down, sit down,' said Dawn sharply. 'Don't stand on ceremony. These fellows are policemen,' she added by way of explanation to her husband. 'I've told them that we gave all the details to the other two yesterday afternoon, but they seemed to want to come in anyway.'

Peter nodded silently. Spence wondered how it must feel to be in your early twenties and be hen-pecked already; there was no doubt about who wore the trousers in this house.

'Well,' said Dawn, who still had not sat down herself, 'would you like a cup of coffee?'

'No thanks,' said Spence. 'Not just now.'

'Sherry then?'

Spence shook his head with a polite smile.

Dawn flicked the hair out of her eyes once more. 'Oh,' she said. 'Well, in that case I hope you won't mind if I do.' She crossed to the sideboard and poured herself a generous glass from a bottle of Bristol Cream. Spence waited until she had sat down again before he began.

'Well now,' he said, 'Detective Inspector Laurel and I are well aware that you were interviewed by two constables yesterday afternoon. And I wouldn't want you to think that there's any special significance attached to this visit. It's a standard practice of ours to see most people who are connected with a murder inquiry at least twice. It's surprising what they remember when they put their minds to it.'

Dawn said nothing and sampled the Bristol Cream. Spence took out a notebook with a smooth plastic cover and put it down on a coffee table beside him.

'Have you any children?' he asked, looking at Dawn.

'One,' she replied.

'How old?'

'Two and a half. She's having a sleep at the moment, thank God.' She pulled her sweater down, further emphasizing her bustline, and lit a cigarette.

'Well now, Mr Stenning,' said Spence, turning away from Dawn for a moment, 'I believe your first name is Peter, is that right?'

Peter swallowed, nodded, and remained silent.

'I'd like to get a bit of background information from you,' Spence continued, 'just to put me in the picture. . . . How long have you been teaching at Petal Park School?'

Peter interlocked the fingers of both hands and twisted them together anxiously; he was leaning forward, sitting on the edge of his chair. 'Oh, about—er—four terms now.'

'Four terms.'

'Yes.'

'Is it your first job?'

'No. Second.'

'Where were you before that?'

'I—er—I taught at a comprehensive in Ealing.'

'For a year?'

'Yes.'

'Just,' said Dawn. 'I didn't think he was going to last as long as a year at times, but he just about managed to survive.'

Peter made no comment but looked slightly embarrassed.

'What was the problem?' said Spence. 'Discipline?'

Peter licked his lips. 'Yes.'

'Some kids just don't want to learn, do they?' said Spence sympathetically.

'No. No, you're absolutely right there,' said Peter. It was the first time he had put any inflexion into his voice and he obviously had painful memories of that particular year in his life. He seemed greatly relieved that Spence understood how he had felt.

'They were a tough lot,' said Dawn, as if she had decided that she ought to be seen to give some support to her husband. 'The girls particularly. It was no place to start a teaching career, but it was the best job we could find at the time.'

'And with a new baby you must have needed the money,' Spence suggested.

'We certainly did,' said Peter, again with deep feeling.

Spence felt that Peter was beginning to loosen up and he tried to make his questions as friendly as possible. 'You were married at college, I suppose?'

'Yes.'

'Was your wife at the college too?'

'I was,' said Dawn. 'And I'd rather you didn't speak of me in the third person, if you don't mind.'

Spence ignored her and continued to address his remarks to Peter. 'How do you find the girls at Petal Park? I suppose they come from a different social background, and the classes are smaller.'

'Oh yes,' said Peter. 'They are.' The fingers relaxed a little. 'It's a different world. Entirely different. . . . They're willing to learn. They're polite, well-mannered. I really enjoy it here. . . . I thought I might not really. I mean in many ways I don't approve of private education, I think it's a bad thing. But I've achieved a lot more here than I expected.'

Dawn exhaled a huge cloud of blue smoke. 'They're a stuck-up lot, though,' she said.

Peter visibly wrestled with the problem of whether to disagree with her. 'I can't say I've been made to feel out of place,' he said at last. 'I get on with most of the staff very well. And there are two other men besides me. It's not as if I was entirely alone.'

'I see,' said Spence. 'Well, as I've said, that was just to fill in the background for me. But what I really want to know about is your dealings with Roger Parnell. I gather, Peter, that you worked for him on a part-time basis.'

Peter nodded. 'Yes,' he said, 'I did.'

'Tell me about it.'

The young man swallowed. 'Well, it was this time last year. A teacher's salary is not all that marvellous, but I do get quite long holidays.'

'He ought to be out working for the Post Office this Christmas,' said Dawn. 'We could do with the money.'

'It's been a long term,' said Peter carefully. 'I think I'm entitled to a bit of a break. . . . Anyway, to get back to last year. You wanted to know how I got mixed up with Roger. . . . It was just after Christmas and we were hard up, as usual. And there was this advert in the paper about earning some spare-time cash. How you could earn fifty pounds a week at it.'

'Why did you need the extra money?'

'Well, we'd like to buy our own house, you see. This one belongs to the school.'

'But we have to pay rent,' said Dawn. 'And all the bills. It's as cold as an igloo and you should see what we spend on heating.'

Spence again ignored her. 'OK, I get the picture. So you followed up the advert. What then?'

'Well, it turned out to be Roger's home phone number, and as he lived so close he suggested that I go round there and see him straight away. So I did. I didn't know him from Adam then, but I found out later that the school had had a lot of trouble with him earlier on.'

'I see. And he explained the arrangement to you?'

'Oh yes. He was really very good at explaining things. And he was a very likeable person, very easy to get on with. I was a bit nervous at first, but he soon made me feel at ease. . . .'

'He was a pretty good salesman himself, I gather.'

'Oh yes, no doubt about it. I've thought about it a lot since, and I've decided that he was the sort of bloke who adapted himself to people. He sort of adjusted what he said and the way he said it so that people would like him. If he knew that you liked dirty jokes he could keep you going the whole evening, and if he thought you were a serious sort of bloke he would be serious. . . . I had a couple of drinks with him once in a pub, me and another bloke, and Roger was like a chameleon. One minute he was telling really filthy stories and the next he was talking politics.'

There was a snort of mirth from Dawn. She leaned across and poked Spence in the ribs. 'Guess who Roger was telling the dirty stories to,' she said, and hooted with laughter, her hand over her mouth. There was an edge of hysteria in her behaviour but Spence decided that with a bit of luck her interruptions might prove illuminating, so he did nothing to silence her.

Peter paused for a second, distracted by his wife's outburst. 'Well, anyway,' he said, 'that first night Roger explained how it worked, this part-time agency business. His company was advertising bank loans in the local papers, and they were also putting leaflets through people's doors, that sort of thing. So one way and another they were getting lots of inquiries from people who wanted to borrow money—and there are a lot of them around, believe me.'

'And I suppose the agent's job was to follow up the inquiries?'

'Yes.'

'In other words, he gave you the names and addresses, and you just had to go round and see people and explain the scheme to them?'

'Yes, that's right. Of course they had to own their own house to be eligible, because the loan was linked to a second mortgage. At that time I barely understood what a first mortgage was, never mind a second one—but Roger made it all sound very simple and easy. And of course the main point that got me interested was that for every person who signed a contract, the agent got twenty-five quid.'

'Which looked like easy money.'

'Very easy. But of course it wasn't quite as straightforward as it seemed.'

'What were the snags?'

'Well, in the first place you were expected to buy the advertising leaflets from him.'

'How much for?'

'Ten pounds a thousand. Which according to Roger was cost price. He also made out that it was a bargain anyway, because you were likely to get anything up to thirty replies from a thousand leaflets.'

'So you bought some.'

'Yes. A thousand at first, another thousand later. He never missed a trick, didn't Roger. It was months before I realised that the leaflets probably cost him about two pounds a thousand. Anyway, I spent two whole evenings shoving them through letter boxes in Shireport—it was damned hard work.'

'Of which you're not overfond,' put in Dawn.

'And how many leads did you get from that thousand leaflets?' Spence asked.

'Three. Or, at any rate, three that Roger told me about. The leaflets all had the company's name on, you see, not mine, and any replies went straight to his office.'

'What makes you think he may have lied to you?'

'Oh, he often told lies, you realized that after a bit. And what really made me doubtful was that one day he told me he'd got a reply from Freddie Gray, the caretaker at Petal Park School. And Freddie doesn't live in an area where I put out any leaflets.'

'I see. But perhaps Freddie had replied to a newspaper ad?'

'No, he didn't, he told me himself it was a leaflet. So if Roger was misleading some other agent I expect he was cheating on me as well.'

'OK. So Roger was a liar. But let's deal with Roger's general approach first and then Freddie's case in particular. What procedure did you follow in general when you went to see someone who had shown interest?'

'Well, Roger had got it all down to a fine art. He had a couple of training sessions last February. A group of us got together at his office, and he had a printed set of rules for us to follow. He also actually showed us how to do it—acted out the parts. First he played the agent, and one of us played the householder, and then vice versa. He was really very good at it, no question about that. All the rest of us were pathetic, me included. But he showed us how to deal with the kind of questions people ask.'

Spence was pleased with the way things were going; Peter seemed fully relaxed now and was talking freely.

'What sort of success rate did you have when you went out to see real customers?' he asked.

'Well, four people signed up, all told, so I made a hundred pounds out of it. I suppose I interviewed about ten altogether. Most of them were pretty desperate, with debts piling up all around them. They understood even less about the bank-loan business than I did, so on the whole it wasn't too difficult to persuade them to sign.'

'And I suppose at first you felt pretty pleased when somebody signed up?'

'I did, yes. I found it a strain, but I must confess I got a great thrill when I managed to make a sale. And Dawn was pleased too—we spent the commission long before I ever got it. . . . That was another thing—Roger always took ages to pay, and there was always a good reason for the delay.'

'Yes—but you didn't remain thrilled with the situation for very long, I gather.'

'No. You see, the fact of the matter was, it was the sort of business where the more lies you told, the easier it was to make money. And that's what got me down after a bit. After I'd been to a few people's houses I began to realize that most of them needed a second mortgage like a hole in their head. What they really needed was someone to organize their lives for them, to teach them how to handle what money they'd already got. But if you were prepared to mis-

lead them, tell them what a marvellous deal they
were being offered and so on, it was easy. They just
signed up and that was it. They got a loan of enough
money to get them out of their present financial mess,
and then they were committed to paying back huge
amounts every month, someimes over seven years or
more.'

'You're too sensitive by half,' said Dawn. She had
calmed down now and was speaking more thoughtfully. 'Too sensitive by half, Peter. People go into
these things with their eyes wide open. There are lots
of sources of information they can use if they want to
get advice—Citizens' Advice Bureaus and I don't know
what else—and if they don't want to find out the
facts then that's their lookout. . . .'

'Well, that's one way of looking at it,' said Peter.

'It's the only way,' said Dawn firmly. 'If I go and buy
a bag of potatoes at the greengrocer's down the road
I don't expect the manager to come out and tell me
that they're a penny cheaper at the supermarket round
the corner. But that's what you'd do.'

'Yes,' said Peter, nodding his head. 'Yes, that's exactly what I felt I ought to do. I felt I ought to warn
people about the dangers and risks of the contract
they were entering into, and that's why I had to give
up being an agent.'

Spence broke in. 'But there was a specific case,
wasn't there? It was Freddie Gray's experience that
really put you off.'

Peter looked surprised. 'How do you know that?'

'Never mind how I know—just tell me about it.'

Peter sighed. 'Well, one day Roger told me that
he'd had an inquiry from old Freddie, as he called
him. Would I go and see him, since we both worked

at the same place. So I said yes. . . . Went to see old Freddie. He needed three hundred pounds pretty badly and he thought it was a fair deal, and so did I at that stage. So, we sent off the papers. . . . Two months later I think it was, Freddie forgot to make a payment. Or said he forgot anyway. The next thing he knew, he got a letter from the bank concerned telling him that if he didn't pay up immediately they were going to sell up his house. Perhaps I should have explained earlier that Roger's company was only acting as agent in arranging these loans. The money itself came from what they call a fringe bank—in other words, one that nobody's ever heard of.'

'Yes,' said Spence, 'I understand about that. And when he got this letter Freddie showed it to you?'

'Oh, yes. Straight away. He said, "They can't do that, can they?" And I didn't think they could at first, but of course when I looked into the matter I found out they could. And would, too. So I went to see Roger. But he wasn't interested—said it was all between Freddie and the bank. And then when I rang up the bank they were completely unhelpful—told me it was none of my business.'

'And they were right,' said Dawn.

This time Peter ignored her. 'Anyway, by this time I was pretty sick of the whole business. There was nothing illegal about it, it was all quite respectable from that point of view, but I didn't like it, I was no good at it, and I wanted nothing more to do with it. So Freddie and I decided to go and see Miss Brockway. When you make a mistake I always think it's best to admit it, and she's an understanding sort of person—you can ask her things without her making you feel you're some sort of idiot.'

'And Miss Brockway sorted it all out?'

'Yes, eventually. She had a word with the chairman of the governors, Mr White—apparently he's a director of Roger's firm—and he suggested an arrangement whereby Miss Brockway paid off the bank loan herself, and now Freddie pays her back instead of the bank.'

'So as a result of all this Miss Brockway was out of pocket?'

'In a sense she was, yes. Though she'll get her money back in the end. She was very patient, incredibly so really, considering what a hideous mess it all was. I wouldn't have been surprised if she'd sacked me. But she didn't seem to mind at all.'

'Mind?' said Dawn. 'Of course she didn't mind. She knows a mug when she sees one—two mugs in fact. I bet Freddie's wages are even lower than yours, and you both put in God knows how many hours of unpaid overtime. The only thing Bee Brockway would draw the line at would be you feeling up one of her girls—if you did that she'd blow your bloody head off with that shotgun of hers.'

Peter looked reproachfully at his wife and she subsided into silence, sucking fiercely on her cigarette.

'So after that incident,' Spence continued, 'you gave up acting as an agent for Roger Parnell, and you had no further contact with him on that score?'

'That's correct,' said Peter.

But Spence sensed that there was something left unspoken. 'It may be correct,' he said, 'but there's more to it than that, isn't there?'

'Yes,' said Peter. 'You see, I gave up acting as an agent in the summer. But then my wife took it up instead.'

28

Dawn crushed out the stub of her cigarette in an ash-tray crowded with its predecessors. Then she pulled her sweater down around her waist yet again and reached for the cigarette pack beside her; her sherry glass was now empty.

'Perhaps you'd like to tell me about that?' said Spence with a quiet smile. Dawn was turning out to be one of his more useful sources of information.

Dawn struck a match and inhaled before replying. 'Well,' she said, 'we're living in an inflationary age, as you may have noticed. Prices go up every week and salaries go up once a year if you're lucky. It seemed to me at the time, and it still does, that the opportunity Roger was offering was altogether too good to miss.' She waved a hand towards Laurel. 'That settee your friend is sitting on—two hundred and fifty quid. And I didn't buy that out of the housekeeping. Or the Bristol Cream either.'

'So you operate in the same sort of way as your husband did,' Spence suggested.

'More or less. Except that I got rather better terms out of Roger than Peter did.'

'In what way?'

'Well, in the first place I got Roger to give me an

exclusive territory—the western half of the county. Any leads that come in from the area are mine and no messing about, whether they're from newspaper ads or anything else.'

'How did you persuade him to give you that?'

'He was only too pleased to, once he found out that I could deliver the goods. But I'd read all Peter's literature, I'd heard him talk about the sort of questions people ask, so it wasn't too difficult. After I'd signed up the first three leads Roger gave me, just like that, he couldn't do enough for me. I've averaged about one case a week since then.'

'And you get a bigger commission,' said Spence, as if stating an established fact.

Dawn looked slightly taken aback, but agreed with him. 'Yes. Fifty quid a case, which still leaves a very handsome margin for Roger's firm, I may say. It could be more than fifty for a really big loan, and I don't have any bloody nonsense about paying for my own leaflets, or putting them through doors myself. Roger fixes all that for me—or did. I'm really sick about him getting killed. Really sick.'

'That'll be the end of a profitable sideline, I suppose?'

Dawn shook her head. 'Oh no. No, there are lots of other firms in the same business. And in some ways it's a convenient way out. I'll deal direct with the bank in future. I know the Area Manager—he's really rather a sweetie—and if I play my cards right I think I can get him to give me the agency for the county. With Roger about that wasn't really possible, so in some ways him getting killed is a blessing.' She stopped suddenly and for the first time looked as if she regretted something she had said.

'Well,' said Spence, 'I think you've told us just about all we need to know, really. Other than the inevitable question—what you were doing on the night of the murder.'

'Not that you suspect us or anything like that,' said Dawn. 'You just want to know if we saw or heard anything unusual.'

'That's right,' said Spence amiably.

'That's what your boys said yesterday, and we didn't believe them either. But we did tell them.'

'Tell me again,' said Spence.

'Well,' said Dawn wearily, 'Mr Universe here stayed at home all evening baby-sitting. He sat in front of the TV for most of the time and then went to bed with a book. A really swinging evening.'

'Is that correct?' Spence asked Peter.

'Yes.'

'You didn't hear or see anything unusual?'

'No.'

Spence turned to Dawn again. 'What about you?'

'I was out from seven-thirty onwards. I went to Marlby to interview two possible clients. Signed one up, lost the other, and had a drink in a pub. I started back about ten-thirty, but the van broke down about three miles from anywhere. I had to wait an hour and a half for the AA to come, an hour for the man to make the bloody thing work again, and then I came home. I got back about one-thirty in the morning. . . . The AA man will vouch for me, I'm sure. He spent more time looking at me than he did at the van, so he's sure to remember.'

Spence nodded. 'Were you awake then?' he asked Peter.

'No.' Peter shook his head. 'I stayed awake until

about one o'clock—I was pretty worried about Dawn
—but then I dropped off.'

'Why were you worried about her—didn't she
phone?'

'No,' said Dawn. 'We haven't got one. They charge
so much to put a phone in that we've always managed
without, but we'll have to get one now. If I'm going
to take over from Roger it'll be essential.'

'I see. All right, last question. Have either of you
ever bought a pair of cuff-links made out of a Roman
coin?'

Peter looked blank. 'No,' he said, 'I can't say I have.'

'What about you?'

'No,' said Dawn.

'Did either of you ever see Roger Parnell wearing
cuff-links of that type?'

They both shook their heads. Spence stood up.
'Right, well, that's it then.' He made for the door
with Laurel following. 'Oh—' Spence paused as he was
about to go out into the hall. 'Just pass me my notebook, would you?'

Peter Stenning reached across, picked up the plas-
tic-covered notebook from the coffee table and handed
it over.

'Thanks very much,' said Spence.

Out in the car Spence promptly slid the notebook
into a polythene bag to protect it. 'Sneaky way of
taking someone's fingerprints,' he said, 'but it saves a
little time.'

Laurel chuckled. He started the car and headed it
down the drive towards Petal Park School. 'You fancy
him then, do you?' he asked.

'Well, to some extent. They make an interesting

couple. She's a lot more extrovert than he is. And I bet she regrets making that mistake when she was still a little bit green.'

'What, getting pregnant you mean?'

'Yes. At least I think it was a mistake. She may have wanted to get her hooks into Peter for some reason, but I rather suspect she got caught after a party. But whether I'm right about that or not, she's grown up a lot since then. He hasn't, of course—he's still very much Mummy's boy.'

'If I was in his shoes I'd be wondering if the baby was mine.'

'Exactly,' said Spence. 'That's what gives Peter a motive, and that's why I took his prints.'

'Hold on a minute—that's not what I meant. The baby couldn't have been anything to do with Parnell —they didn't even know him in those days.'

'No, I know they didn't. But just think about it. For the past six months Dawn Stenning has been working as a part-time agent for Roger Parnell—and that means she's been seeing him at least one night a week.'

'Allegedly on business.'

'Allegedly is right. Now, I never met Roger Parnell, but obviously he was a much more positive character than Peter Stenning. He had good looks, bags of charm and pots of money. As men go he must have been twice as attractive as Peter—and nobody is more painfully conscious of that fact than Peter Stenning himself.'

'So you reckon Peter must have been jealous?'

'Of course he must,' said Spence. 'If he's any kind of a man at all. Can you see Roger Parnell keeping his hands off those neat little tits? I can't. And can you see Dawn Stenning spitting in his eye when he made a pass at her?'

'No,' said Laurel, 'you're right.'

'All of which adds up to a very good reason for Peter Stenning to cave in Parnell's skull.'

'He could have done it all right,' said Laurel thoughtfully. 'She's got an alibi, but he hasn't.'

'She's supposed to have an alibi,' Spence corrected him. 'But I'll do a job card just in case and get her story checked with the AA. If she really was out at Marlby when Parnell was killed then she's in the clear. But her husband definitely isn't.'

29

A few moments later Laurel brought his car to a halt in a parking space near the front door of Petal Park School. It was the first time Spence had been close to the building in daylight, and he decided that the estimate of a hundred and fifty years old which he had made in the dusk the previous evening was about right. It was a handsome four-storey house in red brick, with a flight of steps leading up to the main entrance.

Laurel had parked his car beside a dark-blue MGB GT saloon; he nodded towards it as he and Spence walked towards the steps leading to the front door. 'Miss Brockway's,' he said.

Spence grunted in acknowledgement, and as he did so the front door swung open and Miss Brockway herself came down the steps. She was wearing her brown suede jacket again, this time with dark-brown slacks beneath it; she seemed in a hurry.

'Give her a smile, man,' said Spence out of the corner of his mouth. Then, in his normal voice, he wished Miss Brockway good morning.

'Oh—good morning, Superintendent,' said Miss Brockway cheerfully. She paused as she came level with them. 'Did you want to see me?'

'Yes,' said Spence, 'but I shan't need to detain you. I only wanted a few words with your caretaker, Mr Gray. I imagine he's somewhere about?'

'Yes, he's in the dining-room. He's doing a spot of redecorating—it's long overdue, I'm afraid.'

'And it's all right if we go in and speak to him?'

'Of course,' said Miss Brockway. 'Just go straight in, the door isn't locked. Go down the corridor on the right and take the first door on the left.'

'Thank you,' said Spence.

'Goodbye now,' said Miss Brockway.

'Goodbye,' said Spence and Laurel together. They turned and went up the steps to the front door as Miss Brockway started her car. 'A fine-looking woman,' said Spence with a glint in his eye, but Laurel refused to bite. They paused at the top of the steps and watched as Miss Brockway reversed the MGB out of her parking space and accelerated smartly down the drive. Then Spence turned the huge brass handle and opened the heavy front door.

They went into the entrance hall and as they did so Vera Leigh appeared on the stairs.

'Ah, Superintendent,' she said. 'I was hoping you would call and I saw your car draw up from upstairs. I've got something for you.'

'Oh?' said Spence. As Miss Leigh approached he was struck by how much more confident she seemed today compared with yesterday; she looked quite cheerful, with a healthy glow on her cheeks.

'Yes,' said Miss Leigh. 'I've just come back from a walk over the playing fields with Goldie—nothing like a good brisk walk to blow the cobwebs away—and while we were out Goldie found something. I think it might interest you. I left it here by the front door in case you dropped in.'

She crossed the stone floor of the entrance hall and picked up an object wrapped in newspaper.

'Here,' she said, putting it on a nearby window sill and unwrapping the newspaper. 'It was lying by the fence behind one of the houses in Petal Park Avenue —not too far from Parnell's place. Goldie sniffed at it and barked, so naturally I had a look. . . . What do you make of it?'

Spence peered over Miss Leigh's shoulder. The object on the window sill was a piece of metal, probably cast iron, about nine inches long. It was heavily rusted, as if it had been lying in the grass for some time. It had obviously been made for a specific purpose but off-hand he couldn't imagine what it was.

'It's not a pleasant thought,' Miss Leigh went on, 'but let's face it, if Parnell was clubbed to death this could be the weapon that was used—couldn't it?'

'I'm inclined to doubt it,' said Spence. 'But it was kind of you to bring it to our attention. I wonder what it is?'

'I can tell you exactly what it is,' said Laurel. 'It's a tool supplied with a particular brand of solid-fuel boiler—I used to have one myself. By the look of it it was discarded some time ago, probably when one of the houses in Petal Park Avenue had more sophisticated central heating put in.'

Miss Leigh looked disappointed. 'Oh. So it's probably not the murder weapon after all?'

'Almost certainly not,' said Spence. 'But we'll take it along with us anyway. Did you touch it?'

'Only with my gloves on.'

'Good, because that reminds me of another point. I

wonder if sometime today you and Miss Brockway would call at our London Road police station and let us take your fingerprints.'

Miss Leigh frowned. 'What on earth for?'

'It's just for elimination purposes.'

Miss Leigh was clearly not pleased. 'Oh, very well. If it's going to help you, we will, of course. But it seems quite unnecessary to me.'

'We saw Miss Brockway on the way in,' said Spence, picking up the iron bar in its newspaper covering, 'and she gave us permission to have a word with your caretaker, Freddie Gray. I believe he's in the dining-room.'

'Yes, that's right,' said Miss Leigh. She pointed. 'First door on the left.'

'Thank you,' said Spence. He and Laurel headed for the corridor she had indicated, and Miss Leigh went back upstairs.

Winter sunlight flooding through a tall window illuminated an empty noticeboard on the left-hand wall of the corridor, and beyond that was the half-open door of the dining-room. Spence pushed the door fully open and stepped inside. Even during the school holidays the place seemed to smell of a mixture of stew and fish, as if the aroma from thousands and thousands of meals had soaked into the walls.

Freddie Gray was standing on a pair of steps on the far side of the room; he had almost completed painting the ceiling and only a small area in one corner remained. He glanced at the two police officers as they came in and then looked back at his work.

'I shan't be a minute,' he said. 'But I must just finish this corner. If I stop now it'll show. Not many people would notice, but I would, and it would worry me.'

'Carry on,' said Spence. 'I wouldn't want to spoil a good job.'

Spence cast his eyes round the dining-room. The long tables with chairs pushed under them were all covered with dust-sheets to protect them from the emulsion paint going on to the ceiling. The walls were lined with the inevitable photographs of winners of inter-house hockey competitions, individual tennis champions, and all the other battles of adolescence. Above the photographs were boards painted with the names of the members of the triumphant teams, some of the names in black, some in red; going by his recollections of his own schooldays Spence decided that the names in red were those who had been awarded their colours. He tried to remember what it felt like to regard that sort of thing as important.

'Shan't be a minute,' said Gray again. 'But they don't make ceilings like this nowadays, you know. Look at this plasterwork—all this detail. You couldn't get the men to do it these days. Craftsmanship, that's what it is.'

Gray was nervous, Spence decided. He looked at the hand that held the paintbrush and noticed that it was shaking slightly.

'You'll be from the police, I suppose,' Gray continued after a moment.

'That's right.'

The caretaker nodded. 'Miss Brockway said you might come. She told me not to worry about it or anything—just that you were going round seeing everybody and that sooner or later you'd be seeing me.'

'Quite right.'

Gray put down the small paintbrush he had been

using for the intricate work and took up a four-inch brush for the remaining area of the ceiling. He was a skinny little man, about five feet six, Spence judged, and probably aged about fifty. He had sandy hair, thinning out at the front, and a face that was sprinkled not only with natural freckles but with odd specks of white paint; his teeth were not his own.

Gray's clothing was simple and practical: he was wearing a grubby white one-piece boiler suit that he had evidently used to paint in for about fifteen years; beneath it Spence could just see a shirt with blue stripes and no collar; it seemed several years since Spence had seen anyone wearing a shirt with a detachable collar, but presumably a few elderly gentlemen were still buying them and eventually passing them on to jumble sales.

The painting was suddenly finished and Gray exhaled heavily. 'There,' he said. 'That's done.' He came down the steps and wiped his hands on a rag; then he pulled the dust-sheets off some chairs and they all sat down.

'I suppose you have to be a jack of all trades in this place?' Spence began.

Gray nodded. 'You certainly do. Electrician, plumber, carpenter, the lot. Costs too much to contract it all out, you see. Still, if you're busy then your job's safe, that's what I always say.' His eyes moved quickly from Laurel to Spence, hoping for a friendly grin or an affable reply, but neither seemed willing to help.

'How's the wages?' asked Spence.

'So-so.' Gray licked his lips and paused. 'You've heard, I suppose?'

'About what?'

"Well . . . about me and Mr Parnell. The bank loan and all that.'

'Yes,' said Spence, 'I've heard. But I'd like to hear you tell it as well.'

Gray scratched the back of his head and sighed. 'Well,' he said, 'they say you live and learn, and it certainly taught me a thing or two, I'll say that. I wouldn't want to go through all that worry again, I can tell you. My missus reckoned I nearly had a nervous breakdown and I reckon she's right. I get terrible stomach-ache even now, just thinking about it.'

Spence did not want to hear about the man's stomach-ache. 'I suppose you were hard up after last Christmas, was that the start of it?'

'Yer that's how it started. Christmas, then the car broke down, and then the colour telly went on the blink. And I was behind with the payments already. Well, a bit behind, not much. . . . Course, for me, I wouldn't bother, I can do without all that, but when you've got a wife and kids you have to think of them, don't you? I mean you've got to spend a bit at Christmas for their sakes. And then my youngest, Deborah, she's mentally handicapped, that's the problem. And if my wife didn't get out of the house at weekends I think she'd go bonkers, so that's why we need a car. And what with Deborah not being able to look after herself the wife can't get a job, you see. And Deborah really loves that telly, that's the one thing that keeps her amused. She really loves it, you know?'

'Yes, I can understand that,' said Spence. 'It sounds to me as if you needed the money more than most. Three hundred pounds, wasn't it?'

Gray nodded. 'Yer.'

'And then you saw an advert in the paper offering bank loans.'

'No, I didn't—I got this leaflet through the door. I was standing there in the hall putting my coat on when someone popped it through the letter-box. I never showed it to the missus, she never knew anything about it. Not that she'd have understood it any better than I did, but that's all water under the bridge. Anyway it said, "Bank loans for house-owners", with a slip to send in, so I did. And the next thing was, Mr Stenning came up to me to tell me about it, about three days later.'

'Did he see you here or at home?'

'Here, at the school.'

'And he explained it all to you, did he?'

'Yer. . . . Well, he did, and then again he didn't. I mean he asked me if I understood it, and naturally I said yes. But afterwards, as things turned out, I hadn't really understood it at all. All I knew was that I could get three hundred pounds on the HP, so to speak, by paying back so much a month. I could afford the payments, so it seemed all right. I mean anyone would think the same, wouldn't they?' His eyes appealed for confirmation.

'I gather that an awful lot of people are in the same position,' said Spence. 'Did you realize that Mr Parnell was involved at the time?'

'Oh yes, Mr Stenning told me. And naturally I thought it was a good thing, didn't I? I mean, Mr Stenning seemed a decent sort of bloke, and he certainly did his best for me later on. And Mr Parnell was well known.'

'Well known for what?'

'Well, they reckoned he was a bit of a lad with the

girls, but then he's got an MP for a partner, so naturally you'd expect him to be offering a fair deal, wouldn't you? I was very shocked when I found out what it was really like, very shocked indeed.'

'What went wrong?' said Spence.

'Well, nothing happened for a month or two. But then I was a couple of days late with a payment. I actually made the payment, that was what niggled me, but I was a couple of days late, see, I admit that. I had to wait for pay day. And then the very next morning, by return post, mark you, I got this really snooty letter telling me that if I didn't pay up immediately they were going to sell my house.'

'Which you worked very hard for.'

'Cor, I should say so. My Dad owned his own house and when he passed on I did the same. I used the money he left me to start buying my own. My old Dad didn't believe in council estates and neither do I.'

'I see. . . . What did you do when you got this letter?'

"Well, I showed it to Mr Stenning as soon as I could. And he went as white as a sheet. He got on the phone straight away—one break-time it was, in the summer term—rang the bank and asked them what it was all about, but they told him to get stuffed. So that evening he went round to see Mr Parnell.'

'And what did he say?'

'Nothing. Well, he said he wasn't interested, that was the long and the short of it.'

'How did you feel about that?'

'Terrible. Really terrible. You've heard about people seeing red, well, that's what I did for a minute, I really went wild when Mr Stenning told me. I didn't believe that just being late with a payment could lose you your house. I just didn't believe it.'

'So you went round to see Parnell yourself.' Spence stated it as a fact.

'Well, yes.'

'And then you took a swing at him.' Another fact.

'Mmm.' Gray confirmed it reluctantly.

'But I don't suppose that got you very far.'

'No, you're right, it didn't. He just ducked and then hit me one in the eye—knocked me flat on my back and cooled me off a bit.'

'Did he hurt you?'

'No, not really, no. He was quite nice about it, really. After a minute he picked me up off the floor, sat me down and called me a silly bugger. "Go round and see Bee," he said, "she'll get you off the hook." That's Miss Brockway you know, everyone calls her Bee. "If you're really worried," he said, "go and see Bee, but don't come bothering me because it's none of my bloody business. You're a big boy now," he said. "You went into this thing with your eyes wide open, and if you didn't like the look of it you shouldn't have signed." Which was fair enough, I suppose.'

'And did you see Miss Brockway?'

'Oh yes. Me and Mr Stenning went to see her together. I couldn't go on my own because I didn't understand what it was all about. All I knew was that somebody in London was going to take my house away from me unless I did something pretty quick.'

'And what was done about it?'

'Well, Miss Bee asked a lot of questions, and Mr Stenning had all the papers, and they went over them together. And eventually they worked out some sort of an answer. Miss Brockway paid the bank in London, and instead of me paying them back every month, the school takes it out of my wages instead.'

'So in other words, Miss Brockway did you a favour?'

A slight hesitation. 'Well, yes, I would say so. Yes.'

'But not everybody thinks so.'

'Well, my wife says that if the school had paid me decent wages in the first place we'd never have needed to borrow money, and we wouldn't have got into the mess we did. She reckons Miss Brockway's getting me on the cheap, you see. But I don't agree with that. I know Miss Brockway as well as anyone, and she's not getting rich out of being headmistress. She's a very nice person. She did me a good turn when I needed one and I won't hear a word against her.'

'She has her critics, of course. People talk about her behind her back.'

'Oh yes.'

'What sort of things do they say?'

'Oh. Well—you know.'

'No, I don't know. Tell me.'

'Well. . . .' Gray shuffled on his chair. 'You know. There's the usual catty talk from some of the staff. People always grumble about the boss, don't they?'

'And?'

'Well, you find a few people with dirty minds. Not so much in the school—outsiders. People who think she's a bit too fond of the girls.'

'And is she?'

'Not in the way they mean, no. I don't think it ever enters her head. She's got a heart of gold where the girls are concerned, and that's the truth. I could tell you the names of some of our girls who've got into trouble—you know the sort of thing, babies, drugs, suicide attempts—I'm thinking of one girl in partic- ular now, and believe me, nothing was too much trouble for Miss Brockway. She did everything that could have been done for that girl and then some, right to the very end, and precious little thanks she got for it, so I hear. And you could multiply that ex- ample ten times over. But you see she's a single woman, and so's Miss Leigh, and there'll always be talk from people with nothing better to do. And of course I take a bit of stick too, you know.'

'Oh—who from?'

'Oh, the blokes in the pub mostly. I got a bit of a black eye when young Parnell hit me, and one or two of 'em made out I'd had my eye to the changing- room keyhole. That sort of thing. And the girls pull my leg a bit too, if they see me chatting to one of the pretty ones. I get on well with the girls here, you know—very well indeed. There's no snobbery here, I've never been made to feel small. Miss Brockway won't have any of that.'

'Did you ever see Roger Parnell snooping round the girls' changing rooms?'

Gray seemed genuinely surprised at the idea. 'No, I can't say I did.'

'Where were you the night before last?'

Gray was startled. He had just got used to one line of questioning and now here was another. He rubbed his chin and said nothing.

'Well?'

Gray grinned unconvincingly. 'I thought you might ask me that,' he said. 'My missus wanted to know the same thing. How'd you like that? My own wife wanted to know where I was when a murder was committed.'

'And what did you tell her?'

'Well, I was in the pub, wasn't I? Having my two pints. I'm rationed these days, you know. Went home at closing time and slept like a baby—always do these days.'

Spence grunted. 'Hmm. What about Miss Leigh?'

'What do you mean, what about her?'

'Has she got a heart of gold too?'

'Well, no, I have to be honest there. Not to the same degree. She's nice enough, I suppose, if you get on the right side of her, but moody—you know what women are?'

'Oh yes,' said Spence. I've met a few. . . . Do you wear cuff-links, Mr. Gray?'

'Cuff-links? No, can't say as I do.'

'Do you own a pair of cuff-links?'

'No. Not that I can think of. Bit fancy for me, cuff-links are. I usually roll my shirt sleeves up, to tell you the truth.'

Spence rose to his feet. 'Well, it's back to work now, Mr Gray. You'll just have time to finish the walls before Christmas.'

30

'Where to now?' asked Laurel.

'Back to Parnell's house,' said Spence. 'I've arranged to meet his cleaning woman there at eleven-thirty, and we're late already.'

Laurel put his car into first gear and headed down the drive again. 'There's such a thing as being too honest for your own good,' he said, with a backward nod of his head towards the school.

'What, you mean Freddie Gray?'

'Yes.'

'Possibly. . . . Or perhaps he just wanted us to think what an honest, open fellow he was.'

'I don't think he's clever enough for that,' said Laurel. 'Do you think he's a likely suspect?'

'Oh yes. He's got a first-class motive, has Gray, and he had sense enough to realize that we know about it before we saw him.'

'Well, I can understand him feeling pretty cheesed off with Parnell,' said Laurel. 'By his own admission he went round there last summer and had a violent row with him. But that was months ago—if he did kill Parnell why should he have waited till now to do it?'

'Resentment,' said Spence. 'It boils up, you know.

Having his eye blacked by Parnell can't have gone down too well. And then he got his leg pulled about it in the pub. And now it's Christmas again—he's probably just as broke today as he was last year. Mix all that together with a few pints of beer, which his wife rations for him, and you have an A-1 recipe for murder, no doubt about it.'

'His alibi's a bit dodgy,' said Laurel. 'Home in bed with the wife. Perhaps we ought to get his finger-prints?'

'Good idea,' said Spence. 'I'll do a job card when we get to Parnell's house. And we'll get someone to go round and see his wife, too. They seem to have had occasional disagreements—perhaps they'll dis-agree about what time he got home that night.'

Laurel turned the car into Petal Park Avenue, and almost immediately they saw Mrs Meadows waiting patiently by the gate of Roger Parnell's house. Laurel drew up in the road and he and Spence escorted Mrs Meadows up the short drive towards the front door.

Mrs Meadows was a ponderous, slow-moving lady, and she carefully walked round the spot where Par-nell's body had been lying the day before. She put a handkerchief to her face as they went into the house, and as they stood in the hall she sobbed quietly.

'This is obviously distressing you,' said Spence. 'Would you like to sit down for a minute?'

'No, no, I'm all right,' said Mrs Meadows. 'I'm sorry to be a nuisance.'

'You'd better sit down anyway,' Spence insisted, and fetched her a chair. 'It's bound to get you down a bit —after all, you'd known Roger since he was a child.'

Mrs Meadows obediently sat down but shook her

head in reply to Spence's comment. 'It's not Roger I'm crying about,' she said tearfully. 'Though it ought to be, I know. . . .'

'It's your son then,' said Spence.

Mrs Meadows raised her head to look at him. 'Yes,' she said after a moment. 'It's our Teddy.'

'What's the problem with him?' Spence tried to make the question as sympathetic as possible.

'Well, I'm worried to death about him. Worried about what you'll do to him.' She wiped her eyes with her handkerchief.

'I don't think we're going to do anything to him,' said Spence. 'Why should we?'

'Well—he's been in trouble with the law before, you know.'

'Yes, I know that,' said Spence. 'But so what?'

'You're bound to pull him in,' said Mrs. Meadows. Two large tears ran down her cheeks.

'I shall have a check made,' said Spence. 'But that's inevitable. I'm checking up on everyone and everything. Someone will go round and see him and ask him a few questions, that's all. But at this stage I've no reason to suppose that your son is involved in anything serious.'

Mrs Meadows paused for a moment. When she did speak her voice was barely a whisper. 'What time was Roger killed?' she asked.

'About half past midnight,' said Spence. 'As near as we can tell. Why?'

'It couldn't have been earlier than that?'

'No. But why do you want to know?'

'Thank God for that,' said Mrs Meadows. 'Thank God for that.' She stood up and wandered absentmindedly down the hall; then she turned to face them again. 'I've been worried to death about Teddy,' she said. 'Worried sick. He came in late on Tuesday night you see—well, nearly midnight, that's late for us. And he'd got blood on his jacket. When I asked him about it he said he'd been in a fight in a pub, and of course I believed him. Ticked him off, but I believed him. Well I would, wouldn't I? He's my own son. But then on Wednesday morning, when I got home after seeing you, and thought about it, I began to wonder. . . . But if Roger wasn't killed till after midnight then it's all right, isn't it? It couldn't have been Teddy. I made him some cocoa on Tuesday night, after he came in, and he went up and had a bath. I couldn't sleep myself but I looked in on him at about one o'clock and he was fast asleep. So that's all right then, isn't it? Teddy couldn't have had anything to do with it. He was at home when it happened.'

'I never thought he was connected with the murder,' said Spence. 'Not directly. And as I've said, one of my men will probably ask him a few questions today, just as I'm asking you questions, but that doesn't mean we suspect him. . . . Does that make you feel any better?'

Mrs Meadows nodded. 'Yes, that's all right now. It's a real weight off my mind.'

'Well, if you're feeling better,' said Spence, 'I want to start at the top of the house and work our way through every room. And if you notice anything that's missing, or even in the wrong place, I want you to tell me. OK?'

'Yes.'

The tour of the house took twenty minutes and produced little result; at the end of it they all sat down in the living-room.

Mrs Meadows could not vouch for the contents of the two filing cabinets in Roger Parnell's study—he hadn't kept them locked but she had never looked through the papers in them—and she wasn't certain that all the LP records and books were there. But then, as she pointed out, Parnell had often lent people his records or books and had also borrowed some from other people, so there was no telling whether anything was stolen or merely out on loan.

'I see,' said Spence. 'So apart from the odd paperback or record, it doesn't look as though anything's missing?'

Mrs Meadows shook her head.

'The silver's all there?'

'Oh yes, I'd know if any of that was gone, I've polished it often enough. That sugar bowl in the dining-room, for instance, Mrs Parnell always said that I could have that if anything ever happened to her. But Roger never said anything about it, so she couldn't have told him or put it in her will or anything. And he wasn't mean, he would have given it to me if he'd known, but I didn't like to ask.'

'Tell me about his visitors,' said Spence. 'People who came to the house when you were here doing the cleaning.'

'Well, there weren't any really,' said Mrs Meadows. 'I was on my own most of the time. Roger would be out at the office and I'd just get on with it. . . . He had plenty of people in here in the evenings of course—I used to spend half my life emptying the ashtrays. And Mrs White used to come every Tuesday morning, but that would be when I was next door, doing for Mrs Thomson.'

'How do you know about Mrs White coming?'

'Well, I used to see her, didn't I? I'd be upstairs doing the hoovering next door, and I'd see her arrive about nine o'clock. And then leave about eleven.'

'And this happened every Tuesday morning?'

'In the winter it did, yes. In the summertime Roger used to go round to her house and swim in the pool. . . . I've got a friend who lives in our street who does some of the cleaning for Mrs White, and she told me about that.'

'I see. Was there any gossip about it, these regular Tuesday morning visits?'

'Well, not what you'd call gossip, no. I mean, no one made out they were carrying on or anything like that, she's so much older than he is. I think she just came round to see him out of the kindness of her heart mainly, to see that he was looking after himself properly. She did come one day when I was in here cleaning, and they had coffee together. And then afterwards she helped me to dry up the cups. And she said then to make sure he always had plenty of fresh fruit in the house, that sort of thing. Mr and Mrs White were friends of Roger's parents, you see, years and years ago they were friends.'

'So nobody thought much about this weekly visit?'

'I don't see why they should. It was common knowledge that they were in business together, Roger told me that himself. Mr and Mrs White were directors of his company, she used to bring money round for him, that sort of thing.'

'Money? How do you know about that?'

'Well, once she brought him some money, let's put

it that way. Very occasionally she would come round when I was here, as I've said, on a Wednesday or a Friday instead of on a Tuesday. And once I saw her give Roger an envelope. And I know it had money in it because he opened it and paid me out of it soon afterwards. I expect it was wages for the firm or something like that.'

Spence didn't pursue the matter. Instead he asked Mrs Meadows to accompany him out to the garage to see if she could find anything missing from there. She pottered about for some minutes, peering at the shelves through her glasses.

'A lot of this motoring stuff I can't tell you about,' she said eventually. 'All these plugs and things, they all look alike to me. But there is one thing that was kept in here that I can't see.'

'What's that?'

'Well, years ago, before they had central heating put in, they had coal fires. And one day Mrs Parnell gave me the money to go down to the ironmonger's in London Road and buy her a good strong hammer, to break up the big lumps of coal with. Twelve and six it cost, and I thought it was an awful lot of money at the time. But the hammer's gone. I can't find it anywhere.'

Spence didn't tell her that one of his men had found it in the nearby hedge, covered with blood and hairs from the head of Roger Parnell. But Mrs Meadows must have guessed, for as they drove her home she took out her handkerchief and again began to weep.

31

Once they had delivered Mrs Meadows to her home, Spence and Laurel returned to the London Road police station. There they found their sergeant, Percy Wilberforce, waiting with a clipboard full of information.

'Number one,' said Wilberforce, 'Records cannot identify the prints on the murder weapon. And it officially is the murder weapon now, Forensic have said so.'

'If that's the good news,' said Spence, 'I don't want to hear the bad.'

Wilberforce politely ignored him. 'The victim's business partner, Mr Alec Dane, has been in to see us and the prints aren't his either. Likewise Mr White, the MP, and Mrs White.'

Spence sighed. 'Thanks very much. Try these for size.' He handed over the polythene bag containing the notebook handled by Peter Stenning. 'And a couple more people will be in to give their prints later on today, Miss Brockway and Miss Leigh from the school. Oh—and here's a job card to send someone round to get the school caretaker done. . . . Anything else to report?'

'Yes, sir. Shortly after the fingerprint man had left

Mrs White's place, she rang up. She said that her husband had now gone out for the rest of the day but that she would like to see you as soon as possible to enlarge on this morning's discussion. She particularly asked to see you alone, sir.'

'Oh, did she?' Spence looked at his watch: it was twelve-thirty. 'Right—well you can ring her back and say that I'll call round at half past one.'

'Half past one.' Wilberforce noted it down on his clipboard.

'Any news yet about that taxi-driver who took a girl away from Parnell's house on Tuesday evening?'

'No sir.'

'Why the hell not?'

'Well, taxi-drivers tend to work in shifts, sir. We only started enquiring this morning and most of the blokes who are working evenings this week aren't on duty yet.'

'What's that got to do with anything?' growled Spence. 'They're all radio-controlled these days—the firms ought to have records of who was picked up where at what time and where they were taken to.'

'Some do and some don't,' said Wilberforce firmly. 'We'll keep at it.'

'You do that,' said Spence. 'Let's all do that.'

Spence returned to his office and made his daily telephone call to the Assistant Chief Constable (Crime). With any luck, frequent phone calls would keep the man in Wellbridge, where he belonged. Spence gave the ACC a summary of the progress that had been made since he had dictated his initial report. The ACC listened impassively for the most part but ended the conversation by giving Spence a word of warning. The Chief Constable's daughter, it appeared, had been educated at Petal Park School, and she was not entirely unacquainted with Parnell; she was somewhat distressed by his death. At the top of the chain of command there was therefore rather more interest than usual in bringing the investigation to a speedy and satisfactory conclusion. Consequently, he, the ACC (Crime) himself, would be coming down to see Spence that evening to appraise the situation at first hand.

Thanks very much, thought Spence as he put the phone down. That's all I need, the Chief Constable's daughter breathing down my neck.

Spence took his time over lunch in the canteen. He had decided early on in his career that it was a false economy to try to save time by going without meals or bolting them down in five minutes flat; he had discovered that he functioned much more efficiently on a properly digested meal, and nothing short of a maniac loose with a gun was going to change his ways.

At one-thirty prompt, however, he returned to Petal Park Avenue and brought his dark-blue Cortina 2000 GT to a halt outside the home of Marcus White, MP. He had come alone this time; Laurel had remained behind to confer with his men on the afternoon's work.

Spence got out of his car and was heading for the front door of the house when a woman's voice hailed him from behind.

'Superintendent. . . .'

Spence turned to his left to see Mrs White approaching across the lawn. She was wearing a brown sheepskin coat with patch pockets, and black knee-length boots with platform soles. She looked in much better spirits than she had done earlier in the day.

'Thank you for coming back so quickly, Superintendent,' she said as she drew level with Spence. Her eyes roamed around his face: Spence felt it was some time since a woman had looked at him so directly.

'I'm always prepared to listen to what people have to say,' Spence replied. 'But let me make it quite clear straight away that unless you have something useful to tell me I shall be departing as quickly as I came.'

Mrs White laughed. 'Always the man of action,' she said. 'Never a minute to spare for reflection, have you? Ah well, I'll try to get to the point at once, if that's what you want. But I thought we might take a little walk in the garden, if it's not too cold for you?'

'That's all right with me,' said Spence.

'Good. Well, let's wander round the back and look at the pool.'

Mrs White led the way at a leisurely pace round the side of the house; Spence adjusted his long stride to avoid overtaking her.

'I think I said this morning,' Mrs White began, 'that my husband and I have no secrets from each other. And that's true. But at the same time there are some things which can be said to a third party much more tactfully when one's husband is not present. Do you follow me?'

Spence nodded.

'Now the first point I want to make to you is that I am as anxious as you are to catch the person who killed Roger, though no doubt for different reasons. I am really grieved by his death, Superintendent, really very grieved. Although I'm not sure that that's quite the right word. I haven't sat in my room and wept about him, because I'm not the type. But I resent the fact that he has been murdered. I resent it bitterly, in a physical sense—I can actually taste it in my mouth. . . . The whole thing makes me angry, very angry indeed, and I want to resolve that anger, preferably by scratching out the eyes of whoever killed him. . . . But that's not possible, of course, so I want the next best thing. I want to help you. . . . Now it seems to me that I knew Roger as well as anyone— knew him for years and years and years—and if anyone possesses the key to this mystery, without realizing it, it's me. Assuming, that is, that he wasn't murdered by chance. I take it you don't accept the idea that he interrupted a burglar and was killed more or less by accident?'

'You're right,' said Spence, 'I don't accept that theory at all. It's a possibility, of course, and I haven't discounted it. But my general feeling is that in one way or another Roger offended a lot of people. And whoever killed him did so because they wanted to get their own back.'

'Well, we agree on that at least,' said Mrs White. 'And what I suggest you do is ask me questions. You're the expert, you're the one who knows what information is most likely to be useful. So go ahead—ask. And as we're alone I will give you absolutely honest answers. And trust you to be discreet. . . . How does that sound to you?'

'It sounds promising,' said Spence.

They had reached the open-air swimming pool. It was about fifteen feet wide by thirty feet long, empty now apart from a few dead leaves.

'This is a happy place for me,' said Mrs White. 'Roger swam here many times.'

'Every Tuesday morning,' said Spence.

Mrs White nodded. 'In the summer, yes.'

'And he swam naked, I assume?'

'Of course. We're completely secluded.'

'And what did your housekeeper think of that? She looks rather a puritan.'

Mrs White laughed. 'Oh, she loved it. Absolutely loved it, as well she might. But she would never admit it, of course. She used to watch from an upstairs window, thinking that no one could see. I used to dock an appropriate fee from her wages.'

Spence laughed too, and followed Mrs White round the edge of the pool towards some white-painted metal chairs and tables at the far end.

'How old was Roger when you first made a grab for him?' Spence asked.

Mrs White smiled. 'That's a vulgar question, Superintendent, but a perceptive one. . . . He was fourteen, as it happens. The pool was here when we bought the house, though we had the heating and the filtration plant put in later. And from time to time we used it for social purposes. Young party workers used to come, and a few local children if they were well behaved. Roger came one day with his mother—she was a beautiful person too, though rather a prude. Perhaps that's why Roger reacted. Anyway he was fourteen when I first knew him.'

Mrs White touched the seat of one of the metal chairs to make sure that it was dry and then sat down; Spence joined her.

'He was a very beautiful boy. He was fully mature

at that age and he was well aware of what it was all about. A day or two after he came round here with his mother he was back again on his own. Of course he'd already found out that my husband was away. He knocked at the door, pointed out that it was a very hot day, and could he please have a swim in the pool? Oh, and he was terribly sorry but he'd forgotten his costume, did I mind if he went in without one? Did I mind? Dear God, if he'd brought one with him I'd have ripped it off him in no time at all. So I said yes, and he just nipped indoors through the french windows there, with a wicked grin on his face, and I sat out here. And a few moments later he came out into the sunshine. . . . I don't know whether it's relevant, Superintendent, but I am here to say that seeing that boy come out naked into the sunlight was one of the great moments of my life. In fact *the* greatest, bar none. . . . He was like a Greek god, he really was, he was so beautiful. He didn't have an erection or anything like that, he didn't need to, he was just beautiful. He was, without any question at all, the most desirable human being I have ever set eyes on. And fortunately, praise be to God, he was so disposed that I had a share of him from time to time.'

Spence nodded. 'Once a week, wasn't it?'

'Well, more or less.'

'And,' said Spence gently, 'he cost you money.'

Mrs White smiled. 'Yes, he did, that's quite true. But I've never begrudged spending money. Never. In my time I've spent a small fortune by most people's standards, but I've always known what I wanted and I've always been willing to pay for it.'

'So when you handed over money to him on Tuesday mornings, it wasn't blackmail—it was just that you were paying him for his services?'

'That's right. Though I wouldn't admit it to everyone, of course. And the funny thing was, I enjoyed it more because of that. He would say to me sometimes, that'll cost you five pounds extra, or ten pounds extra, and because of that it made it all the better. Some of the best times of my life cost me an extra ten pounds on a Tuesday morning, and the experience was cheap at the price.'

'Tell me how it started, this payment business.'

'Oh well, it was when he was at school first of all. I think right from the beginning he saw me as a source of income, because let's face it, I am no Helen of Troy. But he liked me too, you know. We couldn't possibly have had a relationship for so many years if I hadn't been able to satisfy some deep-felt need of his. Though you may find that hard to believe.'

'I don't find it hard to believe at all,' said Spence. And that was an understatement. Mrs White's face would never have launched even one ship, but Spence was in no doubt that she had one of the most powerfully sexual personalities he had ever come across.

'So he sort of borrowed a pound or two when he was at school,' Spence continued.

'Yes, that's right. He would say that he was a bit hard up this week, until his mother came up with the next instalment of his allowance, and could I tide him over. And I suppose his mother, being a widow, did find it a bit difficult to make ends meet.'

'And as he got older, his needs became greater?'

'Naturally. But I still didn't mind. I handle my own financial affairs—it's the only actual work I do, but I like to think I do it pretty well.'

'And then finally, after university and a year or two's experience in London, Roger approached you for capital to start his own business?'

'It wasn't only a question of capital. . . .'

'But of your husband's name as well.'

'Exactly. Marcus's name opens a few doors. Not as many as Marcus would like to think, but that's true of all of us, I suppose.'

'And how did Marcus feel about becoming involved with young Parnell?'

Mrs White chuckled. 'He wasn't entirely enthusiastic.'

'But you persuaded him.'

'Yes. Marcus agreed to become a director of Roger's firm in the same way that one does many things. One doesn't always want to invite the Bishop to dinner, because he is a bore of the first order, but ones does.'

'Yes, I see. In your opinion then, would it be fair to say that Roger took those photographs of your husband as a kind of contingency plan? After all, if you had fallen under a bus or something, he might well have needed some sanction to keep Marcus on his side.'

'Yes, I think you've hit the nail on the head there, Superintendent. As you say, if anything had happened to me Marcus might very well have severed all links with Roger, and Roger might have found that a bit inconvenient. It looks bad, doesn't it, if a man of some influence and standing quite obviously dumps you.'

'I've heard rumours to the effect that your husband had severe reservations about Roger's business ethics.'

'He had, yes. Marcus has a very well developed sense of political self-preservation. He was never very keen on being tied up with Roger in the first place, and as time went by he became less so. Marcus has problems with the constituency, you see. One or two very influential people round here are very keen on a sense of responsibility in business, the unacceptable face of capitalism and all that sort of thing. Quite frankly a lot of it is half-baked nonsense, although it's not a bad line to take politically. But the people we're dealing with haven't the intelligence to see it as a useful ploy —some of them actually believe what they say. So as Marcus got to know Roger's methods rather better, he naturally became a bit nervous.'

'Did Roger ever do anything illegal?'

'Not to my knowledge, no. He had more sense. But on the other hand he would go so close to the edge of the law that you couldn't get a razor blade in between. Quite right too. I understand that approach, that's the way my family made their money, but the fellows round here who wear the old school tie, they've never quite forgotten all that rubbish they learnt on the rugger field about giving the other fellow a sporting chance. But the world just doesn't work like that, and Roger was no fool—he understood what makes things tick.'

And much good it did him, thought Spence. 'Had Marcus spoken to Roger about his doubts?' he said aloud.

'Oh yes, they discussed it. They were both quite reasonable people. Marcus suggested taking his name out of the business and leaving the money in. Roger's proposal was that we could have the money back tomorrow provided Marcus's name stayed on the letterhead.'

'I see. . . . Tell me, do you and Marcus sleep in separate rooms?'

'We do.'

'So—excuse me for being so blunt—but Marcus could actually have killed Roger? After you went to bed on Tuesday night he could have gone round there to see him, had an argument with him, and lost his temper.'

Mrs White shook her head. 'No, no. I don't blame you for suggesting it, that's your job, but it's a non-starter. That's not the way Marcus works. And in any case he'd had a hell of a lot to drink on Tuesday night. He's got problems with his girl friend at the moment —he's afraid she's falling in love with another man. Money doesn't solve everything, you see. . . . No, Marcus went to bed about a quarter to twelve, and believe me, he could hardly make it up the stairs, much less go round to Roger's place.'

'He could have been putting on an act.'

'No, he couldn't. You can't put on an act which will fool someone you've been married to for twenty-three years.'

'No,' said Spence, 'I suppose you can't. . . . What about you—had you been drinking too?'

'No, I was stone cold sober. But I didn't kill him either.'

'All right,' said Spence. 'If you and Marcus didn't, who did?'

'A woman.'

'What's her motive?'

'Hell hath no fury, Superintendent.'

'Ah, but that's just the trouble—he didn't scorn any of them so far as I can see.'

'Not many, that's true. But some of them must have got very upset when he stopped coming round to see them. Women get possessive, you know—even me, and I think I'm as objective about sex as any woman can be.' Mrs White put her hand into the pocket of her sheepskin coat and drew out several pieces of blue notepaper folded in half. 'I've made a list here of seven women whom I consider to be capable of murder in certain circumstances. I've also made some notes on their possible motives. My suggestion is that you go round and see them and hear what they have to say.'

'Thanks,' said Spence, 'I will.'

He took the pieces of paper from her and glanced through them. The seven names and addresses meant nothing to him at present, but that didn't surprise him; there were no doubt many women in Roger Parnell's life whose names he had yet to learn. And as for having seven suspects, as far as Spence was concerned there were at least eight: he had a list of his own, and Mrs White's name was near the top.

32

As soon as Spence returned to his car the radio squawked at him urgently. He identified himself and was told that Detective Inspector Laurel requested that he return to the London Road police station as soon as possible.

'On my way,' said Spence.

Five minutes later he brought his Cortina to a halt in the car park at the rear of the police station. Laurel was standing in the yard waiting for him, and Spence wound down the window to hear what he had to say.

'We've got a break for a change,' said Laurel. He looked worried but pleased at the same time. 'The prints Peter Stenning left on that notebook he handed to you—they match up with the ones on the hammer. Exactly. . . .' He allowed himself a smile. 'Looks as if it's all over.'

Spence did not smile back. 'I'd like to think so,' he said. 'But I'm not convinced.' He climbed out of his car and paused beside it. 'What have you done about it so far?'

'Well, as soon as I heard that the prints matched up with those on the hammer I went round to The

Lodge and asked Stenning to come and help us with our inquiries.'

Spence grinned. 'What did he do, give you five out of ten for using a cliché?'

'No—he just came like a lamb.'

Spence sighed. 'Yes, he would. That's just the trouble. Where is he now?'

'In your office. Wilberforce is keeping an eye on him at the moment.'

'Hmm. Well, I don't suppose he'd run very far if he was left on his own. Hasn't the heart for it. . . . What have you said to him?'

Laurel looked perturbed by Spence's attitude. 'Nothing much. Just told him that you want to ask him some more questions.'

'You didn't mention the hammer?'

'Christ, no.'

Spence nodded approval. 'Good. Well, let's see what he has to say.'

They crossed the station yard together. Once inside the mobile office unit Spence opened the door to his own office and asked Sergeant Wilberforce to come outside for a moment; then he closed the office door so that Peter Stenning could not hear what he was saying.

'Before I start on Stenning,' said Spence, 'there's something I want to ask you. This girl that was at Parnell's house on Tuesday night. It's about time we had an answer on where the taxi took her.'

'We've got one,' said Wilberforce smugly. 'A driver working for a firm called Radiocabs picked her up at eight-thirty precisely.'

'Yes,' said Spence patiently, 'but where did he take her?'

'Forty-four Linton Drive.'

'And where's that? Show me on the map.'

Wilberforce went into his office and Spence followed him. Laurel stood at the door, looking astonished by the whole conversation. Wilberforce unfolded a street map of Downsea and spread it out on his desk; he stabbed it with his forefinger. 'Here,' he said.

'Hmm. . . . And who exactly lives at forty-four Linton Drive?'

'Two people are on the electoral roll: Arthur William Dane and Susan Lesley Dane.'

'I see—and are they or aren't they?'

'Do you mean are they married, sir?'

'No, I meant are they or aren't they related to Alec Dane, Roger Parnell's office manager?'

Wilberforce blinked. 'Oh. Well, the answer is yes, sir. At the suggestion of the duty sergeant I telephoned the chief clerk of one of the local banks, on the off-chance that he might know. He told me that the Arthur William Dane who lives at forty-four Linton Drive is the father of Alec Dane. He works for an insurance firm too.'

'And Susan Lesley?'

'She is the daughter of Arthur and the sister of Alec.'

'Oh, is she—well, in that case I've met her. She was in Dane's office last night, putting on her make-up before she went to a dance. What about her mother?'

'Dead, sir.'

'Hmm. I wonder what the bloody hell Susan Dane was doing talking to Roger Parnell a few hours before he was murdered? And why didn't she tell us about it?'

'I couldn't say, sir.'

Spence gazed into space for a few moments and then turned and walked past Laurel into his own office, where Peter Stenning was waiting. He went round behind his desk, took off his overcoat and hung it on a peg; then he sat down.

Peter Stenning was perched nervously on the edge of a chair in front of the desk. His knees were together and his hands were folded tightly on top of them; he looked very pale and kept his eyes on the floor.

Laurel also came into the room and sat down behind Stenning, a notebook and pencil held at the ready.

'Peter Stenning,' said Spence slowly, 'you are not obliged to say anything unless you wish to do so, but what you do say may be put in writing and given in evidence. . . . Do you understand?'

Stenning nodded.

'Yes or no?' said Spence.

'Yes.' Stenning's voice cracked in the middle of the word and he cleared his throat nervously.

'Right then—let's get this over with the minimum amount of wasted time. . . . We have a slight problem Mr Stenning. What you told us earlier is at variance with the facts. You told the men who were making door-to-door inquiries yesterday afternoon that on Tuesday night you stayed indoors all evening. You said your wife was out late, until one-thirty a.m., and while she was gone you watched TV, read a book, and eventually went to bed, falling asleep about midnight. You heard, saw and did nothing at all unusual. Now, when I saw you this morning you told me much the same story, except that this time you said you went to sleep about one a.m. But in fact neither version of that story is entirely true, is it?'

Stenning shook his head miserably. 'No,' he said. 'It's not.'

'Let me help you a bit,' said Spence, changing to a more sympathetic tone. 'We're not as hard-bitten as we look, you know. I can understand how your mind was working. . . . Now, your wife went out about seven-thirty, right?'

No answer. Spence raised his voice. 'Is that right?' 'Yes.'

'OK. We both know that she went to Marlby to flog second mortgages. Not a job that you approve of, but there we are. And for a couple of hours, maybe three, no problem. But then, as ten-thirty moves on to eleven, and eleven o'clock becomes midnight, you begin to wonder where the hell she is. Am I right?'

'Yes. Yes.' Tears appeared in Stenning's eyes.

'All right,' said Spence, taking no notice of the tears. 'So, as time goes by, the thought crosses your mind that Dawn has been out to Marlby, she's made a sale, maybe two, and now she's gone back to Parnell's place with the papers. Correct?'

More nods. Stenning put both hands over his mouth to silence the sobs which threatened to emerge, but he was not completely successful; a stifled moan came out.

'And that wouldn't matter,' Spence went on, 'that would be quite normal. She's probably been to Parnell's place to celebrate a sale before, and come back with nothing worse than half a bottle of Bristol Cream inside her. But this time, as midnight becomes one o'clock, this time it occurs to you that she's not just sitting there talking about the weather—that she is, not to put too fine a point on it, in bed wih him. Right?'

A terrible moaning cry came out of Stenning's mouth. His eyes were tightly closed and his teeth were gritted together. He gave several loud cries in an agony of frustration, and banged his fists on his knees. For a moment the reaction shook even Spence, who was used to violent emotions. But then Stenning rested his forehead on the desk in front of him, and after perhaps half a minute the moans subsided and there was silence.

'So,' Spence continued calmly, 'somewhere about one o'clock in the morning, you left your home, left your sleeping daughter, and went over to Parnell's house. . . . Sit up now, lad, and tell me all about it.'

With a huge effort Stenning pulled himself back into an upright sitting position. He took off his glasses, wiped his eyes with a handkerchief, and took several deep, gasping breaths. 'Yes,' he said, 'yes. That's right.'

'You did go over to Parnell's place?'

'Yes.'

'What time was it exactly?'

'Oh, about . . . one o'clock. Just after. . . . I kept setting deadlines, you see, deadlines when I'd do something about it. . . . First it was midnight. Then half past. And finally one o'clock. . . . You're quite right, of course. Dawn often did go over there with papers, or just for a chat. Discussing strategy, she called it. She had big plans, you know—still does, of course. He was going to turn her into a fully-fledged consultant. He said she had great talent. And she has too —great little deceiver, Dawn is.'

'Which way did you go—across the park?'

'Yes, that's right. Across the playing fields, over the fence, and up the garden path.'

'And of course there were no lights on anywhere.'

'No. Nothing. Not at the back anyway.'

'So you broke a window to get in.'

'What?'

'You broke a window to get in,' Spence repeated.

'No, no, I didn't.' Stenning sounded quite resentful. 'I never went anywhere near the windows. Well, yes, I did actually, I put my face up close to the glass to see if the curtains were drawn. But they weren't.'

'You mean you could see into the living-room?'

'Yes.'

'And it was empty?'

'Yes.'

'What did you do then?'

"Well. . . .' He thought about it. 'I waited a bit. I was cold, and I just stood there rubbing my hands together and shivering. And—this will give you some idea of the state I was in—I began to imagine that I could hear voices, whispering. I got really scared, really terrified, and I was going to run. But then I thought no, they're upstairs in the bedroom looking down at me, whispering and laughing, and if I run I shall never live it down. I could picture them standing at the window without any clothes on, him standing behind her with his arms round her to keep her warm, whispering in her ear.' He paused for a long time, reliving the moment in his mind. 'Anyway. . . . Eventually I must have realized that that was all madness. I stepped back a bit and looked up at the windows, and there was nobody there. Nobody I could see anyway. And I decided that the whispering was just the noises in my head that I could hear because it was so quiet. So then I thought I'll go round to the front—they're probably in a room at the front with the lights on, and if I ring the doorbell Dawn will come home with me.'

'And then you went round to the front door.'

'Yes. . . . Funnily enough I wasn't scared any more. I'd pulled myself together. That's the silly thing about me—I get scared by some very ordinary things, but things that would frighten the life out of other people don't worry me at all. . . . I went round to the front of the house and I saw at once that there was someone lying by the front door. It was pretty dark but I could make out the shape all right. So I went over to him—he was lying on his face—and turned him over. And of course it was Roger. . . . Well, I could see he was dead. I mean there was no doubt about that. I've never seen anyone else who was dead, but you can tell all right, even though it was pretty dark, it was absolutely unmistakable. And then just as I was getting up my foot touched something on the ground. I groped around, picked it up, and held it up to what little light there was. And of course it was the hammer. It was all sticky with blood. It wasn't very nice, so I just . . . turned around and threw it away. Threw it as far as I could. There was a sort of crackling sound as if it landed in the hedge.' He stopped talking and stared straight ahead of him.

'And then what did you do?'

Stenning shrugged. 'Went home.'

'The same way?'

'Yes. I didn't hurry. There didn't seem to be any point. Just went in, brushed my shoes on the mat, washed my hands, and went to bed. When Dawn came in I pretended to be asleep.'

'You didn't think of contacting the police?'

'No.'

'Why not?'

Stenning shrugged again. 'No point. He was obviously dead.'

'It wasn't because you thought Dawn had killed him?'

'No, no.' The idea was clearly unthinkable to him. 'Dawn wouldn't do a thing like that. And in any case, she was out at Marlby.'

'Yes. . . . And the next morning, weren't you worried about what had happened, worried that you'd left your fingerprints on the hammer?'

'Well, yes, I was a bit. But not very worried, actually. I was surprised by how easy it was to carry on as normal. When Dawn heard the news from the baker she got quite upset—so I was kept busy one way and another.'

'Didn't it occur to you that if we found the hammer we would suspect you of the murder?'

'No, not really. I mean I thought that even if you found the hammer you probably wouldn't have my fingerprints—and even if you did trace it to me I hadn't done anything wrong.' He looked directly at Spence for the first time, as if seeking confirmation of his innocence.

'Wait here,' said Spence. He got up and went out of the door of the office, motioning to Laurel to come with him. Sergeant Wilberforce was standing guard outside the door, and as Spence and Laurel came out he went in without waiting to be told. Spence and

Laurel went into Percy's office opposite and sat down.

"Well,' said Spence, 'what do you think?'

Laurel took his time about answering. 'Stenning has a motive,' he said eventually. 'Suspected adultery with his wife. And there's not much doubt that the suspicion was justified. And then there are his finger-prints—they're all over the murder weapon. And, last-ly, he admits to going over to Parnell's house at about the right time. It all fits.'

'So it does,' said Spence. 'So it does. But he says he didn't break into the house. Why should he lie about that?'

'I'm not sure why he's lying,' said Laurel. 'But I know why he went in and scattered stuff around.'

'Why?'

'Because the ground floor was in darkness. He broke in and rushed upstairs, expecting to find his wife and Parnell in bed together. But he didn't, there was no one there.'

'I see. Why did he search the files, then?'

'Looking for evidence, evidence of adultery. And in my view he probably found it. It was common knowl-edge that Parnell was a camera bug, and I imagine Stenning searched the files looking for pictures of his wife. I wouldn't be surprised if he found them either, as nude as all the others. And if he did find them, that would have made him violent enough to hang about near the garage, waiting for Parnell to come home.'

'Not bad,' said Spence. 'Not bad at all.'

'If it was up to me,' said Laurel, 'I'd charge him now.'

'Well it's not up to you,' said Spence. 'And we aren't going to.'

Laurel paused and then persisted. 'But we've got

ample evidence,' he said. 'Ample evidence to justify a charge.'

'I agree,' said Spence. 'We've probably got enough evidence to convict him, never mind charge him. But having enough evidence and having the right man are two different things. You see, I believe his story, it's as simple as that.'

'Why do you believe him?'

'Well, because people who find dead bodies do some very strange things. I once had a case where a perfectly respectable woman left her home and kids and went into hiding, just to avoid having to talk about it. So I'm quite ready to believe that Stenning panicked when he found the hammer. And in any case, if I can't tell the difference between a man who's telling the truth and a man who's lying then it's time I retired.'

'But if Stenning didn't break into Parnell's house then who the hell did?' demanded Laurel.

'I don't know,' said Spence. 'And I can't fault your explanation in theory. But I just can't see Stenning as a killer—he's too passive by half.' Spence rose to his feet. 'You'd better go over it all again with him— several times. See if he changes his story, and take a statement at the end of it all. But you'll have to manage on your own, because I'm going out.'

Laurel looked bewildered. 'Where are you going?'

'I'm going to see this girl,' said Spence. 'Alec Dane's sister Susan—the girl who was at Parnell's house on Tuesday night. I want to know why she was there.'

33

Spence took his time about driving to see Miss Dane. He felt in his bones that he was getting towards the end of this investigation, but a murder case was a bit like building a house of cards: in the final stages there was always the danger of ruining the whole thing with one careless move. He deliberately forced himself not to hurry.

Linton Drive was a quiet suburban road with the inevitable rows of semi-detached houses peacefully ignoring each other. The houses looked pre-war, the front gardens divided by low brick walls and occasional hedges. A small group of children moved reluctantly out of the way as Spence drove slowly past, looking for number forty-four. He found it at last, parked, and rang the doorbell. The children resumed playing in the road.

After a few moments the door was opened by Susan Dane. Her dark brown hair was down around her shoulders this afternoon, unlike the night before. She was wearing a white blouse with long sleeves; over the blouse she wore a light grey apron-fronted dress with bands disappearing over the shoulders. Whether intentionally or not, the outfit looked very much like a school uniform, all except for a pair of blue carpet slippers on her feet.

'Good afternoon, Miss Dane,' said Spence. 'Remember me?'

For a second Susan's eyes widened in a flicker of panic; then she regained control, but her expression remained troubled.

'Oh—er—yes,' she said. 'Yes. I remember your face. Last night, wasn't it?'

'It was. Detective Superintendent Spence. I imagine you know why I've come.' He tried not to make it sound too intimidating.

'Oh, yes. Yes, I do.' In true middle-class style Susan glanced up and down the street to see whether any curtains were moving. 'Um—perhaps you'd better come in,' she said.

'Yes, I think that would be best,' said Spence. He gave her an encouraging smile.

Susan led the way into the living-room at the rear of the house and invited Spence to sit down. He did so and rapidly took in his surroundings. The room was small, and seemed rather overcrowded with the traditional three-piece suite. A coal fire flickered gently in the hearth and there was a Van Gogh print on one wall. Everything in the room seemed slightly old-fashioned.

Susan sat down at a respectful distance and leaned forward, her forearms resting on her knees. Spence noticed that her movements were very graceful, although she was obviously a little nervous. 'I suppose you've found out about me visiting Roger on Tuesday night,' she said.

'Yes,' said Spence. He deliberately said nothing

else and waited, but it eventually became clear that he would have to wait a long time, so he went on. 'I was wondering why you hadn't come forward to tell us about it.'

Susan leaned back in her chair. 'Well, I did wonder whether I ought to,' she said. 'I nearly mentioned it last night at Alec's office. But in the end I decided that the conversation I had with Roger was absolutely nothing to do with the murder, so there wasn't really any point.'

'I think we're the best judges of that,' said Spence. 'And it's my belief that your conversation may be very important indeed.'

'But why?' said Susan. 'I thought he was killed by a burglar.'

Spence had to work hard to conceal his impatience; he was getting thoroughly fed up with that story. 'That's one possibility,' he said quietly, 'but there are others. And you ought to have let us know you were there. However, I don't want to labour the point—you'll know better next time.'

'Yes,' said Susan, 'I will.' Spence could see that she meant it. 'And I'm sorry if I did the wrong thing— but I've had an awful lot of other things on my mind just recently. What with my father being in hospital and so on I've had as much on my plate as I could cope with. I hope you understand.'

'What's the matter with your father?' Spence asked.

'He's had a heart attack.'

'Recently?'

'Two weeks ago.'

'Oh—well, if he's made it as far as this then he should be OK, I imagine.'

'Yes, they seem to think he'll make a good recovery now.' She brightened a little at the thought.

'Good. . . . Do you live here alone with him?'

'Yes. My mother died five years ago.'

'I see. And what do you do for a living?'

'I'm a student teacher.'

'Where?'

'At Larkhill College of Education. In London.'

Spence nodded. 'And what about your brother Alec —he's married, I believe?'

'Yes, but he still lives in Downsea. Near enough for me to babysit but not so close that we're on top of him.'

'Very wise,' said Spence. 'Very wise. Did you tell Alec that you'd been at Roger's house on Tuesday night?'

'No. No. . . .'

'Why not?'

'Well—he wouldn't have approved.'

'Why did you go and see Roger?'

'Oh, dear. I was afraid you might ask that. It's rather a long story.'

'It usually is,' said Spence. 'But don't worry, I'm a good listener. And I've got all the time in the world.'

Susan took a breath and began. 'Well, you see, I was at school at Petal Park, for seven years altogether, and I got to know Roger then. We could hardly avoid knowing him really, because every time we had a hockey match he used to come and leer at us. And then four years ago, after he'd been to university and so on, he came back to Downsea to live. And as Alec started to work for him I've heard quite a lot about him since.'

'I see. How old were you when you first knew Roger?'

'Sixteen.'

'And how does this tie up with Tuesday night?'

'Well, when we were sixteen my best friend at that time fell in love with Roger in a really big way.'

'What was her name?'

'Jane. Jane Trent.'

'And she was the same age as you?'

'Sixteen, yes.'

'And I suppose she got hurt?'

'Yes. Yes, she did.' Susan licked her lips. 'It's not easy for me to talk about it because I was so fond of her. . . . But she was a really beautiful girl and she was also a really good girl, kind and generous, not spiteful. She was too good really, she saw only the best in people and that's not always a good thing. . . . But as I was saying, when we were sixteen she fell very much in love with Roger and she spent the whole of that Easter holidays with him.'

'Let me help you,' said Spence. 'As you say, there are some things which it's not easy to talk about. But until she met Roger Parnell and fell in love with him, Jane Trent was a virgin—am I right?'

'Yes.'

'And after the Easter holidays she became pregnant?'

Susan sighed. 'Yes. I suppose you see this sort of thing every day. But it was an enormous shock to me, and in many ways it changed my whole life. . . . As you say, she got pregnant, and as soon as she was certain about it she went round to see Roger and told him. And of course, being the sort of person she was, she assumed that they would get married.'

'But Roger didn't want to know.'

'No.' Susan rested her head on the back of her chair and bit her lip hard; the tears in her eyes seemed on the point of overflowing, but then she blinked them back and went on. 'Now, believe me, I've thought about what happened a great deal over the last three and a half years, and I think in the end I've managed to get it into perspective. And all I can say is that there are two possible ways of looking at it. Either you can say that Roger behaved like an absolute bastard, or you can say that what he did was really quite reasonable. It depends on your point of view. But in any case he made it quite clear to Jane that he regarded her being pregnant as strictly her problem. For all I know he may have warned her before they ever made love that it was her job to make sure that nothing happened—I don't know, I wasn't there. But even if he had said that, she probably wouldn't have taken it in, she was so much in love with him. Or perhaps she actually wanted to become pregnant so that he would marry her and she would have him for ever. I think that's quite possible. She was very unhappy at home, you see, she wanted to get away, and perhaps she thought that was a way to do it. . . . Anyway, the long and short of it was, the whole thing went horribly wrong. She was very much in love with Roger, she was pregnant, and he made it perfectly plain that he wasn't going to marry her. And that he wasn't even in love with her. And to prove it he started going out with other girls, and refused to have anything whatever to do with her.'

'You said just now that Jane was very unhappy at home. Tell me about her family.'

'Well, her parents were divorced. Her mother remarried and went abroad and Jane used to live with her father. But he was always very busy, she hardly ever saw him.'

'Was she a day girl or a boarder?'

'A boarder. Although her father lived in Downsea, still does, and she could have been a day girl quite easily. But I think he wanted to keep her out of the way.'

'OK,' said Spence. 'Now tell me about Jane's reaction to all this.'

'Simple. She tried to kill herself. She discovered overnight that the world wasn't as nice a place as she'd thought it was, and she took all the sleeping pills in her father's bottle and went to bed.'

'Did she die?'

'No. No. . . . I found her in time. This was at the beginning of the summer holidays, and I was worried to death about her, knowing she was pregnant, so I was seeing her every day. When I couldn't get a reply I let myself into the house. They used to keep a spare key in an outhouse round the back. And then when I couldn't wake her up I telephoned Bee and she came round and got her into hospital.'

'Bee being Miss Brockway.'

'Yes.'

'Why did you ring her?'

'I don't know. It seemed a natural thing to do at the time. Jane's father was in London, my father was at work. And Bee had always been very fond of Jane, kept a close eye on her, I suppose because she recognized she was unstable. Bee told me afterwards that it hadn't been a genuine suicide attempt, it was more a cry for help.'

'And did she get any help?'

'Oh yes, Bee did it all. Once Jane came out of hospital Bee went round to see her father. I don't know exactly what was said but I gather she didn't mince words. She took Jane off to London and got her an abortion.'

'Whose idea was that?'

'Bee's I think, but Jane's father paid. She's pretty ruthless is Bee, you know. You may think she's just another schoolmarm, but she just said she wasn't going to have Jane's life ruined by an illegitimate baby and bang, that was it. After the abortion Bee took her on holiday to recover.'

'And did she recover?'

'No, I don't think she ever did. Not properly. Neither physically nor mentally. She was absolutely shattered by the whole thing. That's the whole point I want to make to you, you see. Because of what happened to her, Jane changed completely.'

34

'Tell me what happened next,' said Spence.

'Well, Jane left school, of course, she had to. I stayed on and did 'A' levels for college, and Jane got a job in a boutique. From then on it was downhill all the way. She stopped living at home, because she had terrible rows with her father, and got a place of her own. And she took to drugs, of course. And she got drunk. She was actually arrested for being drunk and disorderly, can you imagine that? The teachers at the school practically died of shame. All except Bee —Bee could forgive her anything. And believe me, Bee did everything possible to help her. She took her to a psychiatrist—in fact two of them, I think. And paid for it herself.'

'But it didn't help?'

'No. Not much. It helped for about three weeks I think, and then it was back to square one.'

'What kind of drugs did Jane take?'

'Anything. Absolutely anything. By the handful, literally. I've been with her in discos and she'd borrow a pound to buy anything that was going, without even asking whether they were uppers or downers, and sink the whole lot with neat gin.'

'So she lost her job.'

'Yes. . . .' Susan suddenly looked sadder than ever. 'You know this story already, don't you?' she asked.

'Not really,' said Spence. 'But I've realized, as you've been talking, that Jane Trent is a girl I have heard about from time to time in this case. The caretaker at Petal Park School mentioned a girl that Miss Brockway had gone out of her way to help, and that must be Jane. And I've heard a lot of stories like hers, of course.'

Susan sighed. 'Yes, well, you're quite right anyway. She lost her jobs, one after the other. And she got pregnant again, if you can believe that—about eighteen months ago. And Bee took her to London again, and paid for the abortion, because by then Jane's father had refused to have anything more to do with her. Jane always went back to Bee when she was really in trouble. She knew there was one person she could really depend on.'

'Other than you, that is.'

Susan's cheeks went pink. 'Well, it's kind of you to say that, but I'm not sure that I could take it as well as Bee. Some of the things Jane used to say and do used to shake me to the core. But nothing could shake Bee, she could take anything.'

'I'm sure she could,' said Spence. 'She's a very strong woman, is your headmistress.'

'Not that she got any thanks for it,' Susan continued. 'When Jane got drunk she used to call Bee the most terrible things—lesbian bitch was about the nicest of them. . . .' She suddenly slumped in her chair. 'I don't think I can tell you any more,' she said. 'It's wearing me out.'

'We're nearly there,' said Spence patiently. 'It won't take long now. . . . Jane started on drugs. Go on from there.'

Susan passed her right hand over her face in a gesture of weariness. 'Well. . . . When I came home from college last Christmas Bee rang me up and told me to be careful because Jane was on heroin. Bee wanted me to know so that I wouldn't do anything silly— you've got to be a bit careful if you're training to teach.'

'But you still went to see Jane?'

'Oh yes, now and then. I couldn't stand it very often, to tell you the truth. You can imagine how she was paying for the heroin, and once when I went to her flat there was actually a man waiting his turn outside the door. Unbelievable. And of course she got VD, and told me about it in glorious technicolour. She seemed to enjoy shocking me. And then in the summer it was all so awful that I had to go and see Bee and ask her what to do. And that helped a good deal. . . . You see, Bee explained to me that Jane was dying. I suppose I should have realized it myself, any sensible person would have done. But I hadn't. Bee said that Jane was dying and that we shouldn't be too upset or too worried about it, because there were some people who just couldn't be helped, no matter how hard you tried. By some accident of fate or up-bringing they were people who couldn't make it. We should never cease to try and help them, but we shouldn't be surprised if, in spite of everything, we failed. And we shouldn't feel guilty about failing, either. . . . I could hardly believe it when Bee told me that Jane was dying. I could hardly believe it. She was only as old as I was, but her life was over and mine was just beginning. . . .' Susan's eyes clouded over again.

'So that brings us to the present,' said Spence gently. 'When did your autumn term end?'

'The tenth of December, the Friday before last. . . . My father had a heart attack on the Thursday evening, but Alec didn't tell me about it till I got home on the Friday. So it wasn't till the Sunday that I thought about Jane at all. When I did, I went round to see her and cleaned out her flat for her. Actually it was a bedsitter by then—she'd moved countless times of course—and it was absolutely filthy. I went round there twice more, and then the last time I went was on Tuesday, the day of the murder.'

'What time?'

'About two o'clock.'

'Was she expecting you?'

'Yes.'

'And you found her dead?'

A long pause. Then: 'Yes. The door wasn't locked. And she was lying on the bed, quite peaceful.'

'You called the police, I hope?'

'Oh yes. . . .'

Spence sensed that there was something else, something she hadn't told him. 'But?' he said.

Susan moved uneasily. 'Well, there's something I ought to tell you that I didn't tell the police at the time. I'm sorry, I realize now that it was wrong. . . . You see, Jane had left two notes, one addressed to me by name and one which said "To whoever finds me". The one which said "To whoever finds me" was just a suicide note. It said "I have decided to kill myself", and she signed it. That's all. The other note, the one specially addressed to me, was longer, but not

very long. It asked me to do two things. First of all it
said "Please tell Roger that I am dead". That was all,
nothing more about that. And secondly it said "Please
give these letters back to Bee, and don't show them
to the fuzz". There were about a dozen letters on the
table with the note, with a rubber band round them.'

'And you didn't tell the police about them?'

'No, I just showed them the first note addressed
to whoever found her, and I put the letters and the
other note in my bag. I did all the right things apart
from that. I was with the police about an hour and a
half, all told.'

'What did you do then?'

'Well, I went home and rang up Jane's father. I
thought it was better that he should hear it from
me than from anyone else.'

'And then you sat down and read the letters.'

Susan looked embarrassed. 'Yes, I'm afraid I did.'

'Don't be ashamed. Jane's note didn't ask you not
to, did it?'

'No.'

'Well then, she obviously had no objection to your
reading them. Were they love letters?'

Susan looked a little flustered. 'No. . . . No, not
really. They were affectionate. She ended up "love,
Bee", and things like that. But they weren't love
letters. There were only about ten or twelve of them
over nearly four years—or those were the ones Jane had
kept, anyway. The first one said how happy Bee was
that they had been able to go away on holiday together—that was in the summer three years ago, after
Jane first tried to kill herself. It said how much Bee
had enjoyed the holiday, that sort of thing. And in the
later letters there was a lot of gossip about the school,

and in every one she urged Jane to look after himself, to try to forget the past, rebuild the future. They were good letters from a good person, I wouldn't want you to think anything else.'

'And then I suppose you did what you'd been asked to do—you returned them.'

'Yes. I had some tea, went to the hospital to see my father, and then I went on to the school.'

'How did you travel?'

'I took a bus.'

'I see. And what time did you get to the school?'

'Oh, about quarter to eight.'

'So Miss Brockway was out?'

'Yes—how did you know that?'

'She went out to dinner about half past seven,' said Spence. 'She told me so yesterday. But I suppose one way or another you were quite relieved that she wasn't there?'

'Yes,' said Susan, 'I was. I was dreading it really, having to tell Bee, and I was quite glad I wasn't able to. But Miss Leigh was in, so I told her what had happened, and left the letters with her.'

'And how did Miss Leigh react?'

'Well, she just said that it was all very sad, but perhaps it was a good thing—at least Jane wouldn't be unhappy any longer.'

'What then?'

'Well, the other thing I'd been asked to do was tell Roger that Jane was dead.'

'So you went round to see him.'

'Yes. After I'd been to the school his house was quite close, so I walked round there. I'm not sure why I bothered, actually. I mean, I knew him quite well when Jane was in love with him, when we were sixteen, but I've hardly seen him since then. But I'd been asked to do it, so I thought I'd better. Jane was a good friend of mine, I felt I owed her that much. . . . She really did love him, you know. I don't think she ever stopped loving him, although she hated him too, of course, for what he did to her.'

'Tell me what happened when you got to the house.'

'Well, I rang the bell. He opened the door. While I was walking round there I'd imagined all sorts of ways of telling him, such as getting very angry and bitter and trying to make him feel ashamed of himself for killing someone—which is what he'd done, in a way. . . . But when it came to it I couldn't do any of that. I just asked him if I could come in for a minute. And he could see I was a bit upset, so he said yes. We went and sat down in his living-room. And then I told him. . . .'

She paused for perhaps half a minute.

'I'll say this for Roger,' she continued, 'he had a knack of adapting himself to you. Whether it was sincere or not I don't know—perhaps it was just a trick. But really I ought to have hated him for causing the death of my best friend—I ought to have scratched his eyes out. But I couldn't, you see. I found myself quite liking him. . . . He told me that he'd half expected to hear that Jane was dead. He said he'd seen her in the street a few times recently and she wouldn't speak to him. But he'd heard all about her, how she was a junkie and a whore. . . . We talked for a bit and he said some quite sensible things. He said he was sorry about the way things had worked out, but that Jane had always had the wrong idea. He said that men were interested in sex and women were interested in love, and that her ideas about love came straight out of women's magazines—which was fair comment I think. And he said life just wasn't like that. I suppose he was right. . . . In the end we ran out of things to say to each other and he called me a taxi to take me home. He paid for it too. So I went home, went to bed, and went to sleep. . . . That's all.'

There was silence for a few moments, and Spence wondered if there was anything he could say to comfort her. After a while he realized that there was.

'It might help you to know,' he said, 'that Roger Parnell was genuinely distressed by what you told him. He spoke to someone about it later on that evening—a nightclub owner called Big Fat Nelly. Do you know her?'

Susan shook her head. 'No,' she said, 'I don't.'

Spence began to add up all the factors in his mind. His thoughts turned to Beatrice Brockway. Now there was a woman who had killed once before when she felt the circumstances justified it: she had shot down a Mau Mau terrorist. Would she be capable of killing a man who had indirectly destroyed one of her pupils—a girl for whom Bee had felt great affection, perhaps love? There was no doubt at all in Spence's mind what the answer to that was. Bee was capable of it, all right. She had motive, means and opportunity: she fulfilled the classic requirements of a suspect.

'Have you a photograph of Jane that I could borrow?' he asked.

'Yes, I have.'

'And have you still got the note that Jane addressed to you? The one you found in the flat on Tuesday?'

'Yes.'

'Perhaps you could get me those two things, then. And could I use your phone while you're doing it?'

'Of course.'

Susan disappeared upstairs, and during her absence from the room Spence dialled the London Road police station. He got through to Laurel. 'Is Peter Stenning still with you?' he asked.

'Very much so.'

'I want you to drive him home,' said Spence. 'I'll be waiting in my car outside The Lodge, and after you've delivered Stenning we'll carry on down to the school together.'

There was a moment's silence while Laurel gathered his wits. 'And who are we going to see there?' he asked.

'Beatrice Brockway,' said Spence. 'Who else?'

35

Spence parked his car at the top of the drive leading to Petal Park School and waited impatiently for Laurel to arrive. It was a quarter past four now, and the dusk was closing rapidly in. On the London Road the street lights were already shining brightly through a thin haze of evening fog.

After about five minutes Laurel drove up. Stenning climbed out and scuttled indoors, and the two cars then hurried on down the drive to Petal Park School. Spence said nothing as he and Laurel approached the front door, and Laurel didn't care to ask any questions.

Miss Brockway herself answered their ring. She seemed surprised to see them yet again, but passed it off with a smile and agreed immediately to Spence's request that they should talk.

'Let's go in the library,' she said, leading the way. 'It's nice and warm in there because we're still trying to complete our stocktake.'

A few moments later, almost exactly twenty-four hours after their first visit, Spence and Laurel found themselves sitting in front of the library fire again.

'There are just one or two points I'd like to go over with you,' Spence began when they were all settled.

He reached into his pocket and took out the photograph which Susan Dane had lent him: it showed Bee Brockway and Jane Trent on a beach in summer. It had been taken during the holiday which Bee and Jane had spent together, three and a half years earlier; they were both wearing swimming costumes, the sun was shining, and they both looked very happy.

Spence passed the photograph over to Miss Brockway. 'The girl you're with in this photograph,' he said. 'Jane Trent. Why didn't you tell me about her connection with Roger Parnell?'

Miss Brockway looked at the photograph for some time before answering, but she remained quite calm. 'The affair between Roger Parnell and this girl was all over a long time ago,' she said. 'I'm afraid it never entered my head to tell you about it.'

Spence chalked up round one to himself; he was never happier than when a suspect started lying, and he just didn't believe that Miss Brockway's last statement was the truth.

'Tell me,' he said, 'are there any other episodes involving Roger Parnell which never entered your head yesterday, but which you think I ought to know about today?'

Miss Brockway blinked at his tone of voice but refused to take offence. 'Superintendent, when we spoke yesterday I didn't give you the details of every separate incident concerning Roger Parnell, because to do so would take up a great deal of your time. Parnell was a compulsive womanizer—he preyed on my girls and he was a thorough nuisance. I thought I'd made that clear.'

'But this particular girl, Jane Trent, was more than just one of the crowd, wasn't she?'

'In what way?'

'Well, you went on holiday with her for one thing. Do you do that with all your girls?'

'Obviously not.'

'All right, then. Jane Trent was therefore someone special. You found her particularly attractive, more so than the average girl.'

Miss Brockway raised an eyebrow. 'I'm not sure that I like the implications of that remark.'

'Well, let me make a direct statement rather than an implied one. It's my belief that you fancied Jane Trent in a big way. You were in love with her.'

Miss Brockway showed annoyance for the first time. 'Absolute rubbish.'

Spence continued. 'Roger Parnell was the man who took her away from you. She was a virgin and he seduced her.'

Miss Brockway went pale. 'That was regrettable, but it wasn't a crime. She was over sixteen.'

'Jane spent all the Easter holidays with him, nearly four years ago now, most of the time in his bed. She fell deeply in love with him—as deeply in love with him as you were with her. After a while Parnell rejected her, and she tried to kill herself. For a while then you got her back. You went on holiday with her. But she relapsed—perhaps she rejected you as brutally as he rejected her. She took refuge in drink and drugs, and she became a prostitute to pay for it.'

Miss Brockway was beginning to crack. There were no tears yet but the shape of her mouth was starting to reflect her pain. 'Now who's being brutal?' she asked.

Spence continued relentlessly. Laurel sat and said

nothing, glad that he apparently wasn't expected to join in.

'Over a period of nearly four years you watched Jane Trent deteriorate,' said Spence. 'She'd been a beautiful, intelligent girl and she became a slut and a whore. She had two abortions, she got hooked on heroin, she had VD. She lived in a filthy hovel, and in the end not even the lowest of the low would pay to have sex with her. And all that was the result of what Roger Parnell did to her. And at last, when you heard that she was dead, you went over there and killed him.'

Miss Brockway gasped, as if Spence had hit her. 'What did you say?' Her eyes stared at him and Spence knew instantly that he had been wrong.

'I said,' Spence repeated tonelessly, 'you went over there and killed him.'

'No, no. Not that. Before.'

'I said that Jane Trent is dead,' said Spence. He paused. 'You didn't know, did you?'

Miss Brockway closed her eyes and groaned. 'Oh God. No, no, I didn't.' Her body swayed for a moment but she pulled herself upright. She gasped again. 'It wasn't unexpected, but I didn't know.' Her shoulders sagged, and Spence continued swiftly before the reaction wiped out her usefulness completely; he had to have confirmation.

'Vera didn't tell you then? On Tuesday night, when you came back here from the Singletons' dinner party, Vera didn't tell you that Jane was dead?'

Miss Brockway shook her head. 'No. No, she didn't.'

'She didn't give you back the letters?'

'What letters?'

'The letters you wrote to Jane Trent.'

Another shake of the head. 'No.'

'And you didn't read about her suicide in the evening paper on Wednesday?'

'No.'

Of course not, thought Spence, remembering now. As he and Laurel had arrived at the school on Wednesday afternoon, Vera Leigh had collected the evening paper from the delivery boy, and had put it into a cupboard in the library.

Spence sighed deeply. 'Well, if it's any comfort,' he said, 'I believe what you're telling me. That's my main problem today, I'm believing what everyone says.'

His mind raced on, working out the implications of what he had been told.

'Listen,' he said, 'this is important. When Jane Trent was at school here, she was a boarder, wasn't she?'

Miss Brockway looked up. 'Yes, most of the time.'

'So Vera Leigh knew her very well—was responsible for her.'

'Yes. In a sense.'

'All right. So where is Vera now?'

'Vera?' Miss Brockway seemed lost. 'Well, she was here a few minutes ago, in the library. I suppose when she heard you arrive and ask to speak to me she went back to her room.'

'And where is her room?'

'Well, she has two. A sitting-room and a bedroom beyond it. The second door down, on the left.'

'Where do you keep the keys to your gun cupboard?'

Miss Brockway looked utterly bewildered. 'Um—in the top right-hand drawer of my desk. But why do you want to know?'

'Is the drawer unlocked?'

'Well, yes, but why?'

'I was afraid you would say that,' said Spence. 'Wait here, both of you.'

Spence crossed the corridor to Miss Brockway's study. He opened the door carefully, not knowing what to expect. The lights were on but the room was empty; the door of the gun cupboard stood open and Spence looked inside: the twelve-bore and the .22 target rifle were both there, but the Smith and Wesson revolver was missing. Spence felt furious with himself for being so slow—if anyone got hurt now it would be his fault.

He left the study and went along the corridor to Vera Leigh's sitting-room. Again he opened the door warily and again the lights were on and the room was empty; so was the bedroom beyond.

On a dressing-table in the bedroom Spence found a pile of letters held together by a rubber band; the top one was addressed to Miss Jane Trent. Beside the letters was a book on archaeology, and on top of the book was a single cuff-link made out of a facsimile Roman coin. Spence almost groaned aloud. In these unisex days he should have thought of the cuff-link falling out of a woman's shirt, especially when the woman concerned had a degree in history. He went back to the library.

'I still haven't found her,' he said. 'Is there anywhere else she could be?'

Miss Brockway's face was white. 'I suppose she might be in the history room,' she said.

'Where's that?'

'Downstairs. First door on the left, past the dining-room.'

Spence nodded. 'I'll find it.'

'Do you want me to call up some help?' said Laurel.

'Not yet,' said Spence. 'I don't think she's gone far. You stay here.'

He went downstairs. The stairs creaked and there was no chance of moving silently. As he went down the corridor past the dining-room he could again smell polish, cabbage and dust.

The door to the history room was ajar and Spence could see that the lights were on inside the room. He pushed the door wide open, aware as he did so that he was a big man and consequently a big target.

Vera Leigh was sitting at the teacher's desk on the far side of the room; her hands were over her face. Bee Brockway's revolver was on top of the desk in front of her.

Spence came slowly into the room and began to walk towards her. Vera quickly picked up the gun and pointed it at him. She looked as if she was quite capable of pulling the trigger and Spence sat down on the nearest chair. After a moment Vera turned the barrel of the revolver away from him and rested it in the palm of her left hand.

'I suppose you've come to arrest me,' she said.

'I'm afraid so,' said Spence.

'I don't think I can stand that,' said Vera.

Spence started to talk at once, to avoid any pauses in which she could summon up her courage.

'I think I can understand how it happened,' he said quickly. 'After Susan Dane called round here on Tuesday night and gave you the news about Jane

Trent, you felt very upset. Naturally anyone would. And Jane had been a boarder—in a way I suppose you blamed yourself for what happened—felt you were partly responsible. And of course you felt bitterly angry with Parnell, because he was the one who corrupted her, led her astray. I can understand all that—policemen are human too, you know.'

He tried to grin at her but it came out lopsided and Vera wasn't smiling at all. Her eyes were wild, staring at him intently. He ploughed on.

'You went over there first when Bee was out. What time, about half past nine?' He willed Vera to answer.

'No.' Her voice sounded hollow. 'More like ten o'clock.'

'I see. Well, you took the gun, I expect. The one you're holding now. You wanted to frighten Roger. Really frighten him. Make him beg for his life, force him to have some kind of understanding of the suffering Jane had gone through. . . . Am I right?'

She hesitated. 'Sort of.'

'But he wasn't there.'

'No.'

'So you broke in, broke a window and opened the french door. You were hoping to find some way to get revenge—something he treasured that you could spoil, or drugs that you could get him arrested for. That was the idea, wasn't it?'

Vera nodded reluctantly.

'So you went through the house, pulling the papers out of the files, emptying cupboards, and you found the photographs of all the girls. You realized then that he'd been taking an even closer interest in the school than you thought. Spying on you.'

'Yes. Yes.' Vera's voice broke. 'They were horrible.

Horrible. . . . I wanted to take them all to the police, straight away, and have him arrested. But then I thought about it, and I realized I couldn't. He probably hadn't done anything wrong—taking pictures isn't a crime. But I had committed a crime—I'd broken into his house. If I went to the police I'd just be in trouble myself. So it was all useless—utterly useless, as usual. So I came back home.'

'And you put the revolver back.'

Vera sighed. 'Yes. Bee would have missed it. She's very careful, very conscientious.'

Spence continued. 'And then Bee came back from her evening out. . . . You talked for a while, and after she'd gone to bed you went over to Parnell's house again. Because you couldn't rest, you couldn't sleep, until you'd actually *done* something, something to level the score, to balance out the unfairness of it all.'

'Oh yes,' said Vera with feeling. 'Yes, that's right. I wanted him to suffer, to feel pain. The police couldn't punish him for what he'd done—not for the pictures, or for Jane. So I wanted to punish him myself . . . I found the hammer in the garage and waited. . . . I didn't want to kill him, of course. Just hurt him. I wanted to fracture his skull. They say that a fractured skull never heals, you know—you have it all your life. And that's what I wanted him to have—a scar to carry through his life, to remind him for ever of what he'd done. . . . But it all went wrong. Dreadfully wrong. It always does.'

She took a deep breath, tightened her grip on the revolver, and moved the barrel upwards towards her head.

'Wait.' said Spence sharply. 'Wait.'

Vera's eyes turned almost sleepily towards him. 'Why should I wait?'

Spence groped for something to say. 'Because life is worth living, that's why,' he said. It sounded so banal that he winced.

'Not for me, it isn't,' said Vera. 'It's horrible and lonely and disgusting. Hideous beyond all description.'

'But we'll help you,' said Spence desperately. 'Bee will help you. She always does.'

For the first time there was a flicker of interest. 'Bee?'

'Yes.'

Vera thought about it. 'Yes, Bee. . . . But I'll go to prison, won't I?'

'You will, yes. But you'll come out,' said Spence. 'It won't be for long. You'll survive. You can make it—I know you can.'

The hand holding the revolver trembled violently; the barrel wavered all over the room.

'Do you think so?' she said.

'I'm sure of it. Certain of it. You're a survivor if ever I saw one.'

Vera paused in a vacuum of silence. Then, slowly, she put the revolver down on top of the desk. She took her hands away from it very carefully. Finally she sighed heavily.

'Well,' she said. 'Perhaps you're right.'